"I would still be down there in that car if you hadn't saved my life."

"Don't mention it." Then Will forced a smile into his voice. "Just act on it. You're going to be my eyes until we get those missiles where they need to be." What he wouldn't give to see her face now. He caressed it instead, feeling a warm wetness on her cheeks that he knew was not river water.

Should he tease her out of this display of emotion or what? That was what he would have done before.

Now he just held her, glorying in the fact that she was alive to cry, to laugh. To kiss.

He found her mouth with his, at first just a light pressure. The he tasted her, encouraging her to open herself to him just a little. Then more fully.

He would never have admitted it before today, but he had wanted to kiss her this way since the day they'd first met.

Dear Reader,

Winter may be cold, but the reading's hot here at Silhouette Intimate Moments, starting with the latest CAVANAUGH JUSTICE tale from award winner Marie Ferrarella, *Alone in the Dark.* Take one tough cop on a mission of protection, add one warmhearted veterinarian, shake, stir, and…voilà! The perfect romance to curl up with as the snow falls.

Karen Templeton introduces the first of THE MEN OF MAYES COUNTY in *Everybody's Hero*—and trust me, you really will fall for Joe Salazar and envy heroine Taylor McIntyre for getting to go home with him at the end of the day. FAMILY SECRETS: THE NEXT GENERATION concludes with *In Destiny's Shadow,* by Ingrid Weaver, and you'll definitely want to be there for the slam-bang finish of the continuity, not to mention the romance with a twist. Those SPECIAL OPS are back in Lyn Stone's *Under the Gun*, an on-the-run story guaranteed to set your heart racing. Linda O. Johnston shows up *Not a Moment Too Soon* to tell the story of a desperate father turning to the psychic he once loved to search for his kidnapped daughter. Finally, welcome new author Rosemary Heim, whose debut novel, *Virgin in Disguise*, has a bounty hunter falling for her quarry—with passionate consequences.

Enjoy all six of these terrific books, then come back next month for more of the best and most exciting romance reading around—only from Silhouette Intimate Moments.

Enjoy!

Leslie J. Wainger
Executive Editor

Please address questions and book requests to:
Silhouette Reader Service
U.S.: 3010 Walden Ave., P.O. Box 1325, Buffalo, NY 14269
Canadian: P.O. Box 609, Fort Erie, Ont. L2A 5X3

Under the Gun
LYN STONE

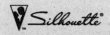

INTIMATE MOMENTS™

Published by Silhouette Books

America's Publisher of Contemporary Romance

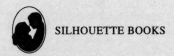 SILHOUETTE BOOKS

ISBN 0-373-27400-9

UNDER THE GUN

Copyright © 2004 by Lynda Stone

Printed in U.S.A.

LYN STONE

loves creating pictures with words. Paints, too. Her love affair with writing and art began in the third grade, when she won a schoolwide prize for her colorful poster for Book Week. She spent the prize money on books, one of which was *Little Women*.

She rewrote the ending so that Jo marries her childhood sweetheart. That's because Lyn had a childhood sweetheart herself and wanted to marry him when she grew up. She did. And now she is living her "happily ever after" in north Alabama with the same guy. She and Allen have traveled the world, have two children, four grandchildren and experienced some wild adventures along the way.

Whether writing romantic historicals or contemporary fiction, Lyn insists on including elements of humor, mystery and danger. Perhaps because that other book she purchased all those years ago was a *Nancy Drew* mystery.

This is for Allen. Thanks for all the resources, suggestions and everything else you provide.

Prologue

MISSION: Olympus
Glenfield, N.J., Nov. 12

"**H**ey, Holly," Will Griffin said into his collar mike as he winked at his brother. "The gig's a wrap. This was the right location, after all. Send the recovery teams over here and sweep up. Matt's calling in his crew."

"Roger that, Will," she answered, her heavy sigh audible in his ear. "Big relief. See you in fifteen."

He cut contact and sucked in a deep, fortifying breath of night air. It stank of cordite mixed with the breeze from a nearby cabbage field.

"That girl's got a bad crush on you, bro," Matt teased. "When are you planning to give her a break?"

Will laughed, adrenaline pumping through his system. "Can't play where I work. Rule number one."

"Aw, man! You better leave her team then and come on back to work with me. Keep wasting time and you'll be too old to do anything about it." He chuckled. "We look enough alike. Think she'd go for me?"

"You lay off Holly."

"Strike the word *off* and it's a deal," Matt quipped.

Will ignored that and deliberately changed the subject. "Wonder why this guy Odin didn't show tonight. He's supposed to be a Cauc and all these guys are foreigners." He glanced at the bodies.

Matt shrugged. "No reason to get his hands dirty doing grunt work, I guess."

Odin was the code name for a mysterious man who supposedly was outfitting a group of terrorists with weapons, in this case a cache of easily transportable missiles and also a crate of submachine guns confiscated off the streets by the local police.

Will looked at the little prop plane he had just exited after checking out the shipment. Surface-to-air Stinger missiles stolen from nearby Picatinny Arsenal filled the passenger section, where the seats had been removed.

Three of the gang lay dead on the runway, another was propped unconscious, cuffed hand and foot, against one of the wheels. There were two more near the delivery truck. They wouldn't be transporting any more SAMs or anything else unless the devil put them to work.

Will checked the nifty little MP5K Heckler and Koch submachine gun slung from the strap over his shoulder. "Barrel's still hot as a firecracker," he muttered as he reloaded.

Matt put down his weapon on the tarmac and started ripping off his Kevlar vest. "I'm sweating like a mule in harness. I hate wearing these damn things."

They were covered head to toe in black. It might be November, but even at 11:00 p.m. it was muggy as hell and felt like the moon was giving off heat. Will yanked his knit mask off and wiped his brow with it.

A movement near the hangar caught his eye. "Down!" he warned Matt just as the figure popped off three rounds. He saw the fire, heard the reports and the thunk as one shot pierced the metal fuselage of the plane. Nine-millimeter handgun, he guessed, whipping up his automatic to sweep the area.

Rapid fire erupted. "God, this is *it!*" Matt cried, and threw himself in front of Will, crashing into him, knocking him flat. Will's weapon spat rounds to one side, striking the aircraft.

This is it. His brother's words rang repeatedly, like thunder in his head, fading slowly to a whisper and then to absolute silence. Matt was hit.

Will tried but couldn't move. Didn't want to. Not apathy, exactly, just resignation. Warm blood oozed across his eyelids.

Matt lay across his chest, heart against heart. Same beat. It felt familiar. Like back in the womb maybe, when they'd been crowded together waiting to be born.

Me first again. The cocky words were Matt's and only in Will's mind, their connection a twin thing long accepted. Will desperately wanted to argue, but something distracted him. Someone was approaching. No sound. No sight. He just sensed it somehow.

He wished it were Holly and the team, but he knew better. There would be no goodbyes. Matt was right. This was *it.*

Chapter 1

Saint Clare's Hospital, Dover, N.J.—November 18

Holly Amberson felt a pain in her chest, an ache of fear and frustration. It was a mere echo of what Will must be experiencing if he had any lucid thoughts at all.

She wished they would airlift him to Bethesda. Newton had been the nearest hospital and their trauma unit excellent, but Will obviously needed more expertise.

"Six days now," she whispered to Jack Mercier, who had just arrived for his turn at Will's bedside. "Other than reflexive responses, nothing."

Jack tightly controlled his expression, but fury mixed with desperation shone in his eyes despite that. "Will's going to come out of this soon, Holly. There's plenty of brain activity."

She nodded and released a sigh. "And some rapid eye movement awhile ago. Dreaming, I guess."

At least he was breathing well on his own, and so far the doctors hadn't ordered a feeding tube. However, another day or so without his regaining consciousness and they would.

Jack nudged Holly's arm with the back of his hand. "Go home and grab a nap. You've got a case in progress and you can't run it with no sleep. Go on back to the motel."

It was standard procedure to have someone on duty whenever a government agent who dealt with special access compartmental classified information underwent medical treatment that required anesthesia, or lost temporary control of his faculties due to illness or injury. Any agent with the appropriate security clearance could be detailed to perform the task, but members of the Sextant team elected to take turns at sentinel duty with one of their own.

The Sextant team, based in McLean, Virgina, was made up of agents that the Director of Homeland Security had recruited from various government organizations expressly for the purpose of preventing or terminating terrorist activities. Holly had been with the FBI. After enlistment in the Marines, Will had worked for Alcohol, Tobacco and Firearms, along with his twin. Jack Mercier, a National Security Agency alumnus, headed up the team.

Three other agents added to the Sextant pool, also drawing on their former resources.

Joe Corda came directly from the Drug Enforcement Agency and had spent three years before that as an Army Ranger. Clay Senate, CIA veteran, remained something of an enigma. Holly reminded herself that she needed to spend a little more time around Clay so she could figure him out. As a natural loner, he seemed to have the hardest time adjusting to teamwork. Eric Vinland, boy genius and resident psychic, hailed from Navy Intelligence.

She called them her Crayola Kids. Three Caucs, a Hispanic, a Native American and her. They had won her heart even before showing such diligence in helping her look after Will.

There was another, much more personal and compelling reason for stationing someone here than simply following intel regulations. There was a chance Will might be able to identify the shooter.

Whoever had delivered the bullet would be a fool not to finish the job, given half a chance. Whatever it took, the team did not intend to let that happen. No one else could be trusted to guard Will as assiduously as they would.

"My report's up-to-date," Holly declared. "Eric's taking over for me. I can stay."

"No," Jack insisted. "Go on, Holly. Get some rest. That's an order."

This was the hardest time of all, leaving. More difficult than staying and watching him, praying for any sign of movement. And that was pure hell.

"The feds come by again today?" Jack asked.

"Yes. And the Military Intel rep and also that ATF guy, Collins, both checked in again by phone. I keep telling them they'll be notified if—when—he comes around. Thank God Will and Matt stopped that plane from taking off. I just hope he'll be able to tell us something significant when he wakes up."

Bullets had riddled the small aircraft, and six of the perps loading it had been shot. But the vehicle that had delivered the stolen cache of weapons to the secluded airstrip and, according to the inventory, three of the shoulder-fire Stinger missiles and launchers were still missing.

"Those things are too damn portable, could take out anything in the air up to five miles away. God only knows where they plan to use them."

"Everybody's on this, Holly."

"All right." She reached out and laid a palm on Will's shoulder. Just a touch.

They each did that whenever they left him. For luck. Or maybe because they might not get the chance to connect with him again if he didn't make it through to their next watch.

Tonight Holly's hand lingered a little longer than usual.

Businesslike, hardheaded, tough-as-nails Holly, who rarely showed any emotion at all, felt as if she was about to cry. Wouldn't that just tear it? Working as the lone female agent on a team of six, she really needed to prove she could bear up under anything without giving way to tears.

Would Will be amused if he ever found out she had such a soft spot?

What if he never came out of the coma? she couldn't help thinking. How could she show up at the office every day and face all those reminders of him?

On every mission, she would be thinking about what he could have added, how great it would be just to pick up her cellphone and punch number three, hear his gruff answer, tease him, make him laugh in spite of himself. God, what she would give to hear his laugh again.

Unable to stop herself even though she knew Jack was watching, Holly brushed back the thick, dark wave of hair that half covered Will's brow. Damage from the bullet, and the surgery to remove it, was healing well.

His hair was too long, she thought, wondering if she should trim it for him tomorrow. It felt damp. Fine beads of sweat dotted his skin.

"It's hot in here," she said, more or less to herself.

Suddenly Will's hand lifted off the bed and struck the side rail with a thunk.

"He moved! Jack, he moved on purpose, I think! Not just a reflex!" she cried. "Will?" Holly leaned over the rail and clutched his shoulder, her fingers buried in the soft folds of his wrinkled hospital gown. "Will, can you hear me?"

Silence dropped like a curtain as Will Griffin opened his eyes and squinted at Holly.

He mouthed the words, "He's coming." She watched his throat work, his dry lips move. "Now. *Armed,*" he whispered forcefully, staring past them, his bloodshot eyes widening, then blinking fiercely.

Was he seeing something they couldn't?

Holly swung around, drew her weapon and planted herself solidly between Will and any threat just as the door opened. Her peripheral vision showed Jack crouched, his SIG-Sauer automatic a deadly finger pointed in the same direction.

The nurse entering the room dropped the IV bags she was holding and crumpled to the floor. The man directly behind her turned and ran.

"Stay with Will!" Jack snapped. He stumbled, then leaped over the fallen nurse and jerked open the door, which had swung almost shut again.

Holly reached through the rail with her free hand and grasped Will's. He squeezed her fingers slightly.

She bit back a sob of relief, adrenaline rushing through her veins.

A few minutes later, Jack returned to the doorway. "He got away. Without a team to search every room on this floor, every supply closet, every stairwell and elevator, we'll never find him! Call security and shut this place down."

He shouted along the hall to the nurses' station, "Get a doctor in here! *Stat!*"

Holly grabbed the phone on the table by the bed and snapped orders to hospital security. She watched Jack crouch beside the nurse who had fainted. Then Holly glanced down at Will.

He seemed to be watching Jack, too, head turned to the side. He blinked hard several times as if to focus better.

She clutched his hand tighter. "The guy split, Will, but we'll get him. Give me a name, hon. That's all we need. Who was he?"

"Dunno," he said with great effort. "Ask...Matt."

Holly winced. Matt hadn't made it.

"Hey, Holly," Mercier said. "Look at this."

"Just a minute, Jack."

Will wouldn't know yet that the bullet that had lodged in his head had first traveled straight through Matt. The perp nearly got a two-fer. But Will *was* going to make it.

He was conscious now, understandably weak but obviously lucid. The bullet hadn't destroyed much tissue, his doctors said. Its velocity had slowed considerably, burrowing through his brother's body.

Will had to make it. The loss of one Griffin was more than their friends could stand. Though Matt had remained with the ATF after Will was recruited to join

Sextant, that had worked to everyone's advantage. Each operative on the new team kept their close contacts from former jobs within other agencies. One didn't get much closer than a twin.

There were several voices behind her now, but Holly didn't worry. Jack was taking care of business. Will was going to need her when he learned what had happened to Matt. She had to decide whether she should tell him straight out.

Instead of giving Will the bad news about his brother, she said, "Don't try to talk anymore, Will. Just stay with us."

She realized she and Jack hadn't even hesitated, hadn't questioned for a minute the urgency Will had projected. They had just responded to the warning and whipped out their pistols. Thank God they had.

Nobody had ever doubted Matt Griffin's extraordinary powers of telepathy. But Will hadn't shared his brother's gift. Not before today, anyway.

Holly linked her fingers with his. His grip was so weak. She hoped against hope that was caused by inactivity and not permanent damage to any response mechanisms. He needed to be strong, much stronger than he was now, when told about Matt's death.

Even as she watched, Will's lips firmed, his expression one of intense pain.

Will knew about his brother. Maybe he had read her face, or perhaps remembered the actual shooting. Holly briefly considering lying to him, assuring him Matt was all right, but she couldn't do it. Didn't think it would do any good, anyway. "I'm so sorry, Will."

His grip tightened perceptibly, as if he were trying to wring a vow out of her.

"Don't you worry," she assured him. "We'll get

that son of a bitch. But you've got to help us. Stay awake if you can. The doctor's on his way. You pull through this, Griffin, you hear me? That's an order.''

She heard a small crowd murmuring behind her and turned to see why no one had disturbed her conversation with Will yet. They should be working over him like bees by now, ensuring that he didn't lapse back into the coma. Adjusting machines, checking his vitals. Something.

''Jack? What's the matter?'' she asked, still holding tightly to Will's hand. She watched a doctor and two attendants trying to revive the nurse. ''Was it a heart attack?'' Holly knew better even as she asked.

Jack left the hubbub and stepped closer to the bed, shot Will a worried look, then frowned. Still he didn't respond to her question. The noisy crew had called a code blue and were loading the woman onto a gurney they had wheeled in.

Only one nurse stayed behind. She began shooing Holly aside, ordering both her and Jack out of the room. Like hell, Holly thought, gritting her teeth, standing her ground gripping Will's hand.

His fingers still clutched hers, stronger now. When he squeezed briefly, the feeling that shot through her promised more than any verbal assurance he might have given.

Something clicked between them in that second, a mental connection. She could clearly feel his determination to pull out of this, his fury and grief over Matt's death, his gratitude for her friendship. His thoughts came through as clearly as if he shouted them out loud.

Despite her constant jabs at the guys about psychic connections, visions, premonitions and such, she was a believer, for sure. But she'd never imagined herself capable of reception. Or of Will being able to project.

A fluke, surely. Comforting and scary at the same time. Even as she thought that, Will relaxed his fingers.

Maybe she had imagined it. That must be it. Despite the fact that her mother was West Indian, Holly knew all her own powers came straight out of books and the excellent training she'd had, certainly not from any inborn woo-woo genes.

Reluctantly she let go of Will's hand and moved away to let the nurse do whatever needed doing.

Holly took Jack's arm and they went to stand in the doorway the others had just vacated. "Will's back with us. He'll stay." She sighed and rubbed her forehead to ease the tingling feeling there.

"Thank God for that," he said vehemently. But he kept his voice low, probably so Will wouldn't hear. "The nurse is dead, Holly."

"Dead? I didn't even hear the pop. That must have been some silencer."

"Didn't use one. Judging by the projectile, I'm sure he was packing spring-loaded plastic. He would never have gotten past security downstairs with anything metal unless he had credentials and a good reason to carry."

"It's a good thing *we* do," Holly whispered. "Can you imagine what would have happened if we'd been caught unarmed?"

He nodded. "The broken ampule was still in the back of her neck." He patted his jacket pocket. "That's what I wanted to show you earlier. They won't guess cause of death until they do the autopsy. Probably not even then, if he used Nicopruss to kill her. It's virtually undetectable. He obviously wasn't expecting Will to have company in here, but you can bet our guy has more than one shot in his pocket.''

"Who the heck was he?'' Holly asked, but they could both guess the answer to that. A hit man. A professional with the right tools.

"Would Odin risk hiring a pro to do this?'' she asked. "It makes sense it's Odin himself, Jack. No one has been able to identify him, and Will probably saw him that night.'' According to the only survivor of the botched raid, Odin had been there in the thick of it, had planned to fly the plane out.

"Whether it's him or not, we're still dealing with a trained assassin.''

"I saw his face,'' she told Jack.

He snapped to attention at that. "I was in a crouch to fire, and the nurse blocked my view. By the time she fell, he was gone. You made eye contact? He knows you saw him?''

Holly nodded again. They stared at each other then, he with concern, she with confirmation of what they both knew. They were definitely dealing with a professional killer, and Holly had just made his list. Will was already at the top of it. Even Jack was at risk. He hadn't seen the man's face, but how could the killer be certain of that?

"We've got to get you out of here,'' Jack said.

"Correction,'' she said with a shake of her head and a worried glance at Will, who was either sleeping peacefully or had lapsed back into his coma. "We've *all* got to get out of here. Now. We're sitting ducks. This guy could have reinforcements stationed out there, just waiting for us to exit.''

Jack already had out his cellphone. He punched in a number and held the device to his ear. "Option three,

Corda. Asap. And bring Solange,'' he snapped, then disconnected. It spoke of how secure this escape was to be that Jack planned to involve his wife, Solange, who was a physician.

The team had worked out plans to cover all contingencies. Holly knew that the third option involved a helicopter on the roof of wing three, four floors up from where they were now.

He put the phone in his pocket. ''I'll get hospital security to help transport Will.'' They would both need to provide cover in case the perp had gone upstairs instead of down. ''You get him unhooked.''

Jack hurried out into the hallway while Holly returned to the bed. Will, eyes still closed, was already fumbling with the tape holding his IV in place. She took over and slid the shunt out of his vein, pressing the area with a tissue to halt the bleeding.

Ice? Had he said the word or had she imagined it? She snatched the top off the plastic pitcher on his bedside table and dipped her hand inside. Tepid water.

She punched the call button. ''Get me some ice in here. Hurry!''

''In a moment, ma'am. We have an emer—''

''Don't you make me come out there with my gun!'' Holly shouted.

Will's lips curved and his body shook slightly.

''You laughing at me, possum? Open those baby grays and look at me.''

''Can't see,'' he grumbled, trying to clear his throat.

''Course you can. You looked straight at me and Jack, too,'' she argued. ''You want sympathy, dude, you're fresh out of luck.''

But one look at the pained expression on his face stole her breath. ''What do you mean, you can't see?''

"Fuzzy," he said, exhaling a rattle of air. "Damn near blind."

"You'll be okay," she assured him, pressing even harder on the tissue. "Now quit bleeding all over the place, will you? I need both hands."

A nurse rushed in carrying another small disposable pitcher. "Here's your ice. Wait! What are you doing? You can't do that!" She attempted to stop Holly's efforts to peel the machine sensors off Will's body.

Holly grabbed her wrist and shook it. "Help me get him unhooked. And close your mouth, girl, you look like a fish. Do what I say."

"But you can't—"

Holly shot her a warning look. The nurse got busy.

"There. All done. You can go now." Holly watched the nurse scurry out. "Little wimp," she muttered.

Mercier came in, a gurney and security guard in tow. "Let's move!" He quickly lowered the side rail of the bed and the guard brought the gurney alongside. In seconds, the two of them had Will loaded on it and were wheeling him down the hall.

Holly took point, on full alert for surprises at each room they passed on the way to the elevator. When it dinged and the door slid open, she crouched and swept the interior, even thought about putting two or three rounds through the roof in case someone was up top. Doubtful there had been time for that, she aimed her weapon at the overhead panel instead, prepared to riddle it.

Slow motion took on a whole new meaning as the elevator rose to the top floor. When they exited into the night air, they still had to wait for the chopper. Holly remained by Will's side, as vigilant as she had ever been, while Mercier quickly swept the roof area.

He returned, declared it clear and dismissed the beefy guard who had come up with them. "Thanks, Charlie. I owe you for volunteering. I won't forget it."

"No problem. Safe trip," the big man said with a toothy grin. "Ma'am. Take care." He turned at the doorway to the roof. "I'll just wait here till the chopper comes and you lift off. Ain't nothin' getting past me." He stationed himself against the heavy metal door and crossed his arms.

Mercier had that effect, Holly knew. He inspired dedication. That's why he was the boss. Apparently even incidental helpers weren't immune to his charm.

Will groaned, drawing her attention.

"Damn it! I should have thought to get him some pain meds." She slapped the heel of her hand against her forehead.

"Here you go," Mercier said. He fished in his pocket and handed her a plastic pill bottle. "Morphine. I'll have to shoulder him into the chopper." There would be no room for the gurney or even a stretcher.

Holly opened the bottle, scooped out a capsule and held it to Will's mouth. "Swallow this."

"No," he said, his voice sounding stronger. "Later."

"Don't be an idiot. Take the pill." She poked it between his lips.

The instant she moved her fingers away, he popped it out. "No."

Holly shook her head with frustration. "Those nurses don't know how lucky they are to get rid of you now that you're awake. Don't make me hold your nose."

His eyes closed, probably against the bright lights now descending. "Later," he mouthed, his murmur drowned out by the *whump whump* of the chopper overhead.

She leaned over Will to shield him from the wash of the blades as the helicopter set down.

Mercier lifted Will to a sitting position, then did a shoulder carry to the open door of the helicopter. Joe Corda, fellow agent and man of many talents who was piloting, gave them a thumbs-up.

Dr. Solange Mercier, Jack's wife, was crouched in the small bay waiting for the patient. She beckoned, and Holly hurriedly climbed in, helping to arrange Will while Jack scrambled aboard.

The instant he pulled the door shut, the slick Bell 206 Longranger rose and curved swiftly away from the tower, shifting the passengers sideways.

"Airborne. Safe," Holly said, knowing no one could hear her over the noise.

Glass on the canopy cracked. "Ground fire!" Joe shouted.

God, this guy didn't give up. Someone was firing at the helicopter—probably with a sniper rifle, given their distance from the ground. Joe zoomed out of range, zigzagging as sharply as the chopper would allow while Jack radioed local authorities below. At least the shooter wasn't using one of those heat-seekers, Holly thought with relief, or they'd be done for.

Stay with me.

Holly jerked her gaze from the holes in the canopy to the patient. Had Will said that, told her to stay? How had she heard him over all this racket?

His eyes were still closed, his mouth pinched. He looked as if he might have returned to the sanctury of silence that had sheltered him these past six day somehow Holly knew he hadn't.

She placed her hand over both of his, now resting on his chest. She'd be right by his side for as long as he needed her, she vowed. This was the mission assigned to her, but that was incidental.

Immediately, it seemed she could feel his inner turmoil decrease, but it probably had nothing to do with her reassuring touch. Solange Mercier had raked away the gown from Will's shoulder and injected him with something.

The chopper droned on, whisking them away from the bright city lights to the sparsely lit suburbs surrounding Dover, then out into the chasm of night to a destination known only to Mercier and Joe Corda.

Holly hadn't even thought to ask Jack where they were going. Where would Will be safe?

The morphine or whatever Solange had administered had cut off Holly's mental connection with Will, if indeed she had really had one. She hadn't realized how strongly she had been feeling whatever it was until it suddenly ceased.

Or, more likely, it was only her imagination working overtime, stimulated by adrenaline that was now draining away.

She pressed her fingers to his wrist and felt the same slow, steady pulse that had blipped on the monitor for six straight days. Only now he had fallen asleep.

Chapter 2

"Where are we?" Holly demanded as soon as Joe set the chopper down and switched off the power. They had been airborne for a little over an hour and a half. In the moonlight, the landscape looked like the backside of nowhere. Coming in, she'd seen a flat field surrounded by trees on three sides, with a driveway that led to a two-lane road.

Now she looked at the ramshackle two-story structure about fifty yards away. It seemed pretty spooky with that lone light shining out the back window.

"Cedar Top Farm, Virginia," Jack announced. "Population six if you count the animals."

Holly glared at him. "This won't do, Jack. Will needs the best medical care he can get. We should fly him to another hospital."

"He'll be safer here. The house is a confiscated property, very recently acquired and outfitted. Not even on official books yet as a safe house, and I'll see that it stays that way. As soon as Will's able to stay awake long enough, you debrief him and contact me with what he knows. There's a secure land line here."

"But Will needs—"

"Time to recover, Holly. Solange has kept up-to-date on his condition throughout his ordeal. His doctors have said all along that once he regained consciousness, he'd probably improve very rapidly. Put that psychology degree of yours to work and help him."

"What if he falls into a coma again?"

"Roanoke's only fifteen miles away. We can get an ambulance out here in less than a quarter hour if he needs it," Jack promised. "He's come out of it, Holly. The main thing we can do for him now is keep him safe and give him time to completely heal, both from his physical trauma and his grief. Protect him from this immediate threat to his life. That's your mission."

"Aren't you staying?" Holly asked Solange. Jack's wife was a physician, a general practitioner, when he might need a neurologist. Still, she was better than no doctor at all.

She shrugged and shook her head. "You can do everything for him that I could. Keep an eye on his vitals, relieve any pain he has with this—Hydrocodone. It might be better for him than the morphine." She handed Holly another pill bottle. "Make certain that he eats enough to regain his strength. Bland food at first. Encourage him to exercise as soon as he begins to feel restless."

"He mentioned his sight. It's fuzzy, he says. He should see a specialist."

"Let me know if that doesn't clear up. We'll fly in someone we can trust," Jack promised. "Meanwhile, make him as comfortable as you can."

Holly nodded, accepting the fact that Mercier had already decided on this course of action—or inaction—and it would be useless to argue.

She stared at the big old Victorian with its peeling paint and tangled shrubbery. A house straight out of a nightmare. She imagined cobwebs, bats and dust, maybe some drug paraphernalia left by former inhabitants.

"We should get him inside." Jack cast a look at Will, who lay motionless. "But I'll go in first, check it out and alert the caretaker."

"Caretaker?" Holly asked as she tucked the blanket tightly around Will to ward off the chill of the night. All he wore was the hospital gown. He looked so vulnerable, Holly wished she could take him in her arms and hold him.

Jack was still speaking, Holly realized. She forced herself to focus.

"Our man here is retired Naval Intelligence. He's been contracted to set the place up with a security system and outfit it as a safe house for DEA, so it's sort of in transition right now. I asked for something off the records and appropriated the place through the highest channels, without offering any details about why we wanted it."

With that pronouncement, he climbed out and went straight to the back door of the house.

Joe had taken off his headset and turned around. "Hey, Will, ol' buddy?" he said softly, his Southern accent more pronounced than usual.

"He's out, but he should be coming around soon," Solange said, shining a penlight into Will's eyes as she lifted his eyelids. She looked up at Holly. "You have some medical training, yes?"

"Worked as a paramedic for a couple of summers

during college." Holly shook her head. "But this…I
don't know, Solange. It's out of my league."

"Call me if you need anything or have any questions," she said, handing Holly a card from her doctor's bag. "My cellphone number. Or call Jack and
he'll find me immediately."

Holly nodded, still wondering if they weren't trusting her entirely too much with Will's recovery. She
was so afraid for him.

Jack had returned to the chopper, bringing their host
with him.

"Donald Grayson," he said by way of introduction.
"This is Agent Holly Amberson."

"Mr. Grayson," she acknowledged.

"Call me Doc."

"Thank God. You're a doctor."

"Nope. Got that tag when I was a medic. First job
after I joined up at age eighteen. Even after I went to
spook school, it just stuck."

Great, Holly thought. Anything he had learned
would be dated by at least thirty years.

Jack interrupted. "The rest of you stay put on the
chopper. We're taking off in about ten. Okay, ready to
transport?"

Holly helped roll Will far enough out of the chopper
for Jack to get a grip on the upper half of his body
while Grayson took his legs. Together they carried him
the short distance to the house. Holly opened the door
and stepped aside, cautioning them to be careful not to
bump him around so much.

Will woke up with a start, his head nearly exploding.
The dryness in his throat reduced his cry to a groaning
curse and he struggled with whoever was holding him.

"Steady now. We'll have you settled in a minute," Mercier said.

Will vaguely recalled there'd been trouble in the hospital. "Put me down. I want…to stand." He had to know if his legs worked. He had to know. "Please," he grunted.

"Not a good idea," he heard Holly say, but they stood him upright, bracing him so he wouldn't fall.

With effort, he straightened his legs and felt his bare feet resting solidly on the floor. It was everything between his feet and his head that gave him problems. His bones seemed to have melted, his muscles reduced to mush. Tingling mush, as if they had all gone to sleep. *Damn!*

"Here's your bed, sir, right behind you. Go ahead and sit down," said an unfamiliar voice filled with concern. It was deeper than Mercier's, not as clipped and forceful, but with the same speech patterns. Will thought he should ask who the man was…tomorrow, maybe. He felt his mind slipping, seeking rest.

A softness caught him, pillowed his aching head. Someone lifted his legs and covered him with a blanket. No, a quilt, he realized as he closed his fingers around the puffy upper edge and felt the stitching.

He drifted back into boyhood. Cool summer nights. Grandmother tucking him in, brushing his hair off his forehead, tapping his nose with her finger. "Morning's waiting on you," he mumbled right along with her, smiling back.

Her soft laugh sounded younger. "So it is. Go back to sleep, Will."

"What did he say?" Jack asked. They had settled Will in and Grayson had left them alone.

Under the Gun

Holly busily adjusted the covers again, even though they didn't need it. "He said 'morning's waiting,' and he's right about that. You'd better take off if you want to make McLean by sunrise." She knew Jack needed to get back to the office, coordinate the team and locate Odin.

"We need to talk first. Come out in the hall."

Holly followed him from the room. She could smell coffee brewing. Boy, could she use some of that. Exhaustion was setting in big time. She followed her nose down the hallway.

Jack held back, his hand on her arm. "You can explain the details to Grayson after we're gone. Just so we're clear, in addition to guarding Will, your orders are to find out if he can add anything to what we know about the op at the airfield, and report to me as soon as possible."

She nodded.

"While he's asleep, you can work up your detailed description and a sketch of the guy in the hospital and get that to us, too. Joe and Clay will have to take over the other cases we've got going, which fortunately are in early stages and not critical. Eric and I will be concentrating on this Odin character. However, if things start popping on this, we'll all be on it."

Holly faced him, hands on her hips. "You think it was Odin himself in the hospital?"

"I believe it was. I'm counting on his coming after me, thinking I got a glimpse of him, too. And I'll be a whole lot easier to find than you and Will."

She leaned back against the wall and closed her eyes.

He grasped her shoulder and gave it a gentle shake. "Do your job, Holly. Let Eric and me do ours. With the SAMs missing and Matt's death and Will's being shot on a multiforce investigation like that, every agency will be solidly behind us all the way. They'll pull out all the stops."

She nodded. "Any communications gear other than the phone line in this firetrap?"

"Everything necessary and then some. I'll be waiting on that sketch."

"My artistic talent leaves a lot to be desired, but I think I can get a fair likeness."

"We'll try to match it with ID photos and get you some to compare. Don't use your personal credit cards while you're here. You have your cover ID with you?"

"Always," she told him.

"Good. You can use that. If Odin's working from the inside, he could have resources to pick up an obvious paper trail."

"You think he's an agent who's flipped?"

"Entirely possible. He found out where Will was." Jack pulled out his wallet and handed her a stack of bills. "Mad money. That's all I have on me, but I'll wire more to Roanoke in Grayson's name tomorrow."

"Thanks," she said as he turned to go. "See you, Jack."

"Soon," he replied.

None of them ever said goodbye. It seemed too final or something, as if they didn't expect to meet again. Funny how they all adhered to that without ever having discussed it.

She followed him to the door and locked it, checked on Will and found him still sleeping peacefully, then went to find the kitchen and that coffee she had smelled.

Grayson offered her a mug as soon as she walked in. "Welcome to paradise," he said with a lopsided grin. "Hungry?"

Holly nodded and he gestured to a plate of sand-wiches on the table. She grabbed one and began to munch, realizing she hadn't eaten anything other than a package of peanut butter crackers since breakfast.

"Got any soup for our patient?" she asked.

"Sure, but he looked like he was down for the count. Want to give me a rundown on what we're dealing with?"

Between bites, Holly outlined what had gone down and why they were here. Then she added, "Chances are there's nothing to worry about. I know you've had training, but I'd like to know if you have any field experience."

Grayson smiled. "Yeah, I do. Anything happens, I've got your back."

He looked capable, Holly thought, as she observed him more closely. She guessed he was around sixty, maybe even older, but seemed in pretty good shape. Not a large man, hardly taller than her own five-five, Grayson moved with the tensile grace of a man trained to strike.

His graying hair was buzzed short in the old military style, the line of it receding just above his temples. His broad features resembled carved mahogany. He wore a dark, close-fitting knit shirt and camouflage pants. His wide feet were bare and heavily callused.

"The way you were looking at that boy in there. He means something to you besides an assignment, right?"

Holly delayed her answer as she drained her mug of coffee and set it down. Then she looked the old soldier square in the eye. "Right. We're on the same team. And we're best friends. Got a problem with that?"

He shook his head. "Don't let's get off on the wrong foot now," he said, holding up one hand as if warding off an argument. "I just hope you won't let personal stuff cloud your judgment if worse comes to worst."

She met his frowning gaze with one of challenge. "My professional and personal objectives are one and the same here—to keep that man alive at all costs. He's very important to me, yes. But he's also vital to the success of future missions."

Grayson pursed his lips and nodded. "I see. You'll keep your head."

"I always keep my head," she replied. But Holly felt a little angry with Grayson for planting the seed of doubt in her mind. Nonsense, of course. Hadn't she remained perfectly detached when Will was threatened in the hospital? Hers had been a textbook response when the shooter appeared.

Will surfaced with a raging thirst. His skin felt like shrink-wrap. "Water," he said, hating the croak that emerged.

A few seconds later, a cool cloth bathed his face. Crushed ice chilled his lips. He opened his mouth, dying to drink something. Anything.

He felt a straw and grabbed it with his lips. The delicious trickle of cold streamed down his parched throat and pooled in his stomach. He seemed aware of every cell in his body soaking it up.

"Easy now," crooned a voice near his ear. *Holly.*

· He reached out to the voice and his palm met her face. He slid his fingers over her cheek, touched her ear, threaded them through her hair.

Holly's was clipped almost as short as his own, lying in little black satin wavelets close to her head. Neat, efficient and sexy as hell. He wasn't supposed to think sexy, not about her, his muzzy brain reminded him.

"Where are we?" he demanded.

"At a safe house not far from Roanoke," she explained, taking his hand in both of hers as she leaned close. "You remember what happened?"

He recalled bits and pieces. There had been trouble. "Some of it," he admitted. "The hospital. A helicopter."

"I'll fill you in on the details later. Just so you know, Solange sedated you. You aren't permanently addled."

Addled didn't begin to describe how he felt. Will turned his head from side to side, struggling to take in his surroundings, but the room was dark. Or he was blind. He remembered the blurriness he had experienced before. "It's night," he said.

"Yes."

"What night?"

"Friday," she told him. "Well, Saturday morning early. About four o'clock. Be daylight soon."

"Holly?"

"Yes, Will?"

"I can't see." He forced the words from between clenched teeth. The thought scared the absolute hell out of him, but he was trained to conceal his emotions. He did so now. No point getting panicked, he told himself. It wouldn't help and might even hurt.

"I know, you told me in the hospital, but your eyes will be fine. It's temporary." A hopeful lie. If she had any basis for it, Will knew she would have explained in detail.

Her voice held a note of desperation. Or maybe not

her voice. That sounded calm enough, now that he thought about it, but he strongly sensed her overwhelming concern. It scared him more that she tried to conceal it than if she'd stated her worry openly.

He forced his lips to stretch into a semblance of a smile. "Thanks for sticking around."

"Now where else would I be, you doofus?" He heard her sigh, a slight breath of sound. She patted his hand.

"Well, I guess you might have to be my eyes for a while. Sorry."

She was talking, but Will stopped listening. All he could think about was getting out of bed and back on his feet. How he would manage that, feeling the way he did, he didn't know how yet, but he would find a way.

There was something he needed to remember, something that haunted him, but his train of thought kept breaking. He hoped to God it was the medication causing the terrible sense of foreboding.

Morning arrived, just as his grandmother had promised when he fell asleep. That had been a dream, he realized now. Grandmother was gone, died when he was sixteen.

So his mind was refusing to function fully at the moment. At least he was aware that it wouldn't, and things seemed to be coming back to him bit by bit.

Sunlight flooded the room, but the shape of objects in it remained nebulous as hell. Colors were fugitive, fragmented.

He rubbed his eyes. Blinking didn't help, either. It was like looking at things through the patterned glass wall tiles that encircled his shower at home.

He fought panic. Before it took hold completely, he sensed he was no longer alone. Holly. She was back.

"Hey, you're awake! Good morning. How's the noggin?"

"A little confused," he said.

"That'll pass. Ready for breakfast? You must be starving."

Her voice sounded too bright, too chipper. She should be ragging him the way she usually did, ordering him around and poking fun, trying her damnedest to make him laugh. That meant he must be even nearer death than he felt, and God knew that was near enough.

He could make out her shape standing just to the left of the foot of his bed. "You look good…in red."

The silence lasted a beat too long. "Thanks."

"You are wearing red, right?" he asked, the question tentative.

"Well, no, not right now. I'm wearing green, but I am holding a red robe. I brought it for you."

"Oh." He swallowed hard, the dryness in his throat much more noticeable. "Thanks."

He felt her settle on the bed beside him. Her arms slid around him and she rested her forehead lightly on his shoulder. "This trouble with your eyes will pass, Will. I know it. I promise…."

"You mentioned breakfast?" he said, gently pushing her away, unwilling to accept what felt too much like pity. That, he could do without.

She moved quickly. He heard her inhale a shaky breath. "Yeah. How about some broth? When you can tolerate that, maybe some Jell-O later. How's that sound?"

He made a face. His appetite was nonexistent at the

moment, but he knew he needed to eat to get his strength back. "How long was I out?"

"Six days," she said, sounding reluctant to discuss it.

He coughed in disbelief. "Six?"

"You were in the hospital. In a coma," she told him.

He remembered the tubes. It was coming back to him now. He shook his head, carefully, because it was pounding so hard he could scarcely think. "A *coma?*"

She touched his arm, wrapped her fingers around it and squeezed. "You were shot, Will. In the head."

He raised his hand and ran it over his hair, found and felt the tender scar just above his right temple. The memory came flooding back all at once. "Matt," he whispered.

She was holding her breath. Then she expelled it. "I'm so sorry, Will. Matt didn't make it."

He had known already, before he asked, but he hadn't wanted it to be real. "You told me before, didn't you?" Why did the randomness of death still surprise him?

"Yes. You have to get well now so we can find that bastard who shot you both. We owe it to Matt. Are you with me?"

With monumental effort, he nodded. Either he was in shock or his subconscious had already accepted Matt's death. He should feel grief-stricken, totally undone, after losing the person closest to him.

Instead, he felt very calm inside, exactly the way he always did immediately before a mission, when he had the objective firmly in place, all the plans worked out. It was as if Matt were in on it with him. He could almost feel the connection.

"Is he…buried?" he asked Holly.

"At Arlington. Full military honors. Marines turned out in force."

That was good. Matt would like that. The Corps took care of its own, even after someone left it.

"We'll go visit him soon," Holly promised.

"When this is over. Not before," Will said firmly. He could not do that until he had avenged the brother beneath that marker. "Our parents?"

"They were there. They visited you in the hospital, too."

"But they're gone again. Back to Italy," he guessed. That sounded bitter. He sighed. At least they had come. Appearances must be kept up.

"You're not alone, Will." Her lips touched his cheek, just a breath of a kiss, a contract sealing her promise. "You'll be okay. Not today, I know, but you *will* be okay."

Maybe, maybe not. But the man who'd killed his brother would be dead one way or another. Sooner or later.

Hours passed in a fog of painful memories and uncontrollable gusts of anger. He forced down the broth Holly brought him and later the gelatin. He sipped what seemed like gallons of ice water. He fought nausea and won. His resolve grew.

A man came in, managed to get him to his feet and walk him to the bathroom and back. Will didn't bother to ask his name. He didn't care who it was.

He focused his whole being on getting back his strength. Unfortunately, that was the only thing he could focus on. That and the fuzzy rectangle of light that was the window.

Blind. Damn it! He held fast to Holly's promise that it was not permanent. He needed to see to find this

Odin. To exact revenge for Matt, to destroy a merciless killer. Will couldn't say goodbye until he'd settled the score. It was all he could do now.

In his mind, he could clearly see his brother nod his approval, hear his voice. *Live for both of us, bro. You know it's what I'd do.*

All right, Will thought, he would do that. Maybe this continued connection he was feeling was not real, but he chose to believe it was. It was too soon to let go completely.

From here on out, no self-pity or survivor's guilt. No time wasted mourning what he couldn't fix. No way would he let Matt down.

Later when he woke, Holly lay next to him, his head cradled on her breasts, her arms around him. This felt good. Right.

He wondered why she had set aside the kick-ass, swaggering attitude he knew so well, and let him see this soft side of her. Her guard was definitely down tonight.

He was sick of that guard of hers, anyway. And his, too.

They had met a couple of years earlier, at Quantico, when they'd attended a special course provided by the FBI for other agencies. She'd been with the Bureau then and Will with ATF. They had hit it off immediately.

Their paths crossed on a joint case a year later, renewing their friendship. He carefully avoided anything more than that. He had taken his cue from her both times, thinking she might be involved with someone else. He had been. Heard she was, too.

Now he and Holly worked together. She was the one

who had recommended him for the Civilian Special Ops antiterrorist team when it was forming, and was responsible for his getting hired for Sextant.

He treated her like one of the guys because that's what she demanded of all the men on the team.

Holly was everyone's little buddy with a bossy mama complex. Every guy on the team would die for her in a heartbeat. She cared about them and showed it, baking them cookies, teaching them to cook, deviling them like a little sister. They adored her.

They respected her, too, he firmly reminded himself. Holly had earned that many times over. She was a damn good agent, one of the best he knew.

Not once had she ever betrayed any stronger feelings for him than the camaraderie they all shared. But now she was lying here holding him in her arms like a lover. How the hell was he supposed to ignore that?

Maybe he wouldn't even try, at least not now when he needed this so badly. He snuggled closer, all but burying his face in her cleavage, drawing in her tantalizing scent, pressing his lips to her satiny skin just above the tickle of lace.

For a few minutes he thought of nothing but the firmness of her well-toned body, the strength in her small frame, the sweet breathiness of her sigh when his lips brushed the swell of her breast.

He fully expected her to pull away, but she didn't. Either she was a damn sound sleeper or their friendship was undergoing a monumental change.

Will valued that friendship the way it was. He envied Holly's easy way with people, her passionate outbursts and her engaging laugh. How did she do it?

She got so *involved.* There wasn't a trace of the ice-princess reserve of the women he went out with. A cautious maneuver on his part, those choices. Safety lay in choosing women like his mother. No danger of emotional entanglements there, that was for damn sure.

Matt had pointed that out and Will had never even bothered to deny it. *Like to like,* he would say. But Will had known since the first time he met Holly that wasn't really so, at least not in his case. Opposites did attract, big time. He also knew he wouldn't act on it.

His head ached. His bones felt like rubber and his muscles like the Jell-O he had eaten earlier. He couldn't believe he was getting aroused, not when he was in this condition. She'd probably smack him if she woke up and realized it.

Not that he would ever do anything to insult her, like coming on to her. He doubted he could follow through at the moment even if *she* were coming on to *him.*

A guilty weariness assaulted him when he remembered how good a friend she had always been to him and how he was seriously taking advantage of that.

Could be that she thought she was merely providing what comfort she could, a distraction from his grief and worry. If so, that was working for the moment, and he would have to thank her for it later.

He luxuriated in the feel of her body warming his and the fact that she cared enough to do this.

Too bad he wasn't up to discovering her motive. He put it on his mental list of things to do right after he avenged his brother's death.

For now, the closeness and caring she offered were enough.

Chapter 3

Will feigned sleep when Holly left his bed so he wouldn't do something crazy like ask her to stay. He suspected her compassion had limits he had come close to violating, and his injury was no excuse.

She returned in a little while and shook him gently. "I'm sorry, Will, but this can't wait any longer. Time for your debriefing."

It angered him that she had turned all professional after lavishing that very personal warmth on him last night. He knew it was an unreasonable response on his part, but he didn't feel reasonable.

His answers were curt as he described all that he recalled from the operation at the airfield.

He remembered too damn little of what had happened that night, and would have given just about anything to forget what he did recall.

The interview proved very short and she left to make

her report. He knew Jack and the others were waiting on it, such as it was.

Somehow, Will had to face this head-on. He had to do all he could to help catch the one who'd killed Matt. But what could he do lying here blind as a bat and mad as hell? He had to get up, get his mind and body in gear and quit hanging on to Holly at every opportunity.

She said he would get over this, that his sight would return. She'd *better* be correct. Right now he wasn't ready to accept any other scenario. He could see a little, make out light and dark. That was something, wasn't it? A good sign. He wasn't totally blind.

Will bumped into a chair, causing a loud clatter when it tipped over on the hardwood floor. He stopped, swaying slightly until he regained his balance.

"What in the world do you think you're trying to do?" Holly cried.

He felt her arms lock around him before he could turn toward her. "I was headed for the bathroom. Do you mind?"

"Yes, I mind!" She shifted to brace her shoulder beneath his arm. "Hold on to me. Go slow. Turn right," she commanded, grunting when he leaned heavily against her.

"Here you are." She placed his hand on the edge of the sink. "You need help?"

"No. I've been doing this all by myself for several years now." She was in a mood? Well, so was he. "You can leave now. I promise not to knock anything else over."

She was still in the doorway. He could vaguely see her move, as if she were shifting from one foot to the other, watching him. "Well? Go!" he ordered.

She moved farther away, but the door still stood

open. Light from the hallway outlined her just
beyond it.

"Planning to aim it for me?" he snapped. "Are
cheap thrills why you're hanging around?"

She scoffed. "Thrills, huh? I've aimed bigger guns
into better places, believe me."

He staggered over and slammed the door in her sassy
face. He felt like hell and she was acting mean as the
devil. He knew his anger was unreasonable and inap-
propriate, but he didn't care right now.

The hook latch on the door was simple enough, even
for a blind man, Will thought. He fastened it and began
feeling his way around the room.

Let her stand out there and fume if she wanted to.
He wasn't leaving here until he had showered and
shaved, and felt at least halfway human again. Maybe
steam from the bath would help, lubricate his eyes or
something. Hell, he'd try anything.

The sound of banging woke him. A loud crash and
rush of air warned him the door had given way. Not a
sound he'd mistake, having busted down a few himself.
Damn, he'd fallen asleep in the tub.

For a second, he considered covering up, but didn't.
He sat there calmly, arms resting on the lip of the enormous antique bathtub, up to his chest in hot, soapy
water. Correction, barely warm, barely soapy water.
How long had he slept?

"Why did you lock that door?" Holly demanded.
She stood above him, probably had her arms crossed,
those long red nails tapping against her sleeves.

He blinked up at her, wishing he could see her expression, even if it was furious. There would be that
sparkle in her dark brown eyes. One thing about Holly,

she looked damn good when she was mad. Her lips might be drawn down, but that accentuated her dimples even more than her smile did.

She would have those two tiny lines between her eyebrows, visible only when she frowned. Otherwise her skin would look smooth as cream with a subtle hint of mocha. And a blush of dusky pink always flared on her high cheekbones when her temper rose like this.

"God, I miss your face," he said, without thinking how plaintive it would sound. He could have kicked himself.

She knelt quickly, her hands covering one of his. "Oh, Will. What am I gonna do with you?"

He rubbed his free hand over his face, dipped it in the water and swiped it again. "Get me a doctor."

"The pain still that bad?" she asked softly.

He shook his head. "No. The eyes are still that bad."

How am I supposed to get Matt's murderer if I can't see to shoot straight?

"I'll help you," she said, as if he'd spoken out loud.

A ripple of unease crawled up his spine. *How did she do that? She'd done it before. When?*

"In the hospital…" She laid her cheek against the back of his hand.

He pulled his hand free and sat upright. "What?"

"In the hospital," she repeated, "you saw something. You envisioned that guy coming down the hall and warned us. If you hadn't, we'd all be dead now. You've never felt…seen anything like that before, have you?"

He was still too shaken to answer, still caught up in the notion that she might be reading his thoughts. As Matt used to do, answering unspoken questions.

What if Holly had the power to do that, too, and had simply elected not to tell anyone about it? Will didn't even want to imagine what she might have picked out of his thoughts about her since they'd first met. No, couldn't be. She would have said something about that, for sure.

As for the other thing she'd mentioned, his warning to them, he didn't want to think about how he had done it. And he sure didn't want to talk about it. Matt could have explained it, if only he were around to ask.

His death seemed unreal, impossible. But it was a fact.

If only Matt had experienced a premonition before they'd gone out that night. He'd had no warning something fatal was about to go down. Why was that? Why hadn't he picked up something—anything—from the shooter before the event? This Odin must have been near enough that Matt could have done so, probably during the whole operation.

Maybe there'd been too many people converging all at once for Matt to have zeroed in on any particular one. After all, just about every man at the airport had been armed and ready to kill anybody who got in the way. And Matt's ability wasn't all that consistent. Not surefire.

He had been blessed—or cursed, as Will sometimes thought—with telepathy and occasionally prescience. Will had never before experienced either one, at least not with people other than his brother.

There was the twin deal, of course. He and Matt had always operated on the same wavelength, a fairly common occurrence between identical twins. Besides that, the best Will had ever managed was the tingling along the back of the neck when being watched, a keen wariness when expecting things to go wrong, the usual intuition many people had.

Life without his twin was just too unthinkable.

Will couldn't decide whether he was now a half person or if he had absorbed Matt's soul and become two. It was as if his brother were still here…even closer than before he had been killed.

"Going back to sleep? If you are, I'm draining this tub so you won't drown," Holly warned, dragging him back to the present. She leaned over the edge and put her hand in the water.

Matt grabbed her wrist, glad to note his reflexes were still working. "You leave the drain alone," he warned. He moved her hand away and promptly turned her loose.

Her fingernail raked softly down the side of his face. "I see you shaved," she said, her tone sardonic.

"How observant."

"Hard not to notice. You have blood running down your neck." Her nail tapped just below where he had nicked himself.

She stood, her figure wavering as he looked up at her. "Come on. Let's get you out of the tub. You're getting all pruny."

Pruny, huh? Maybe his fingers and toes. Will sat right where he was, wondering how many soap bubbles were left in the tub to provide cover. Probably not many. Maybe none.

He was picking up signals from Holly that indicated she was taking full advantage of the view. He felt himself stir. No matter how cold the water, when a woman was looking at you naked, it had a predictable effect.

"Where's that guy? The one who's been helping me," he demanded.

"Doc Grayson? He's in the kitchen. He trained as a medic his first stint in the navy, but he's not a real doctor. He's just—"

"Yes, but he is a real *guy,* okay? Leave me a little dignity. You've already made one too many jokes about my *gun.*"

She laughed, the sound merry as Christmas morning. "You rascal! That dry sense of humor's still working, huh? I'll go get Doc."

Will smiled in spite of himself, listening to her laughter trail down the hallway and out of earshot. It was all right, after all. She wasn't reading his mind. If she had been just now, she wouldn't be laughing.

He splashed water on his face to wash away the blood from the nick.

In a few minutes, someone else entered the room. "Doc...Grayson, is it?"

"That's me," said the quiet, gentle voice. Will sensed he was an older man.

"Thanks for the help."

"No problem. That's what I get paid for."

He didn't elaborate. Doc was a man of few words, his movements unhurried and methodical as he assisted Will out of the tub and helped him dress.

The sweats were new, judging by the slightly starchy feel of them. Will didn't care where the clothes came from; anything was a damn sight better than a freaking hospital gown. He sat down on the john and pulled on the socks Grayson put in his hand.

"Here are your shoes."

One at the time, Will put the stiff new runners on and tied them. This was like being a kid again, but not in a good way. "I'm stronger now." He stood up and stretched. "I feel better," he announced, adding a little starch to his voice. Just saying it almost made it so.

"Take it easy now," Grayson advised. "Don't want to get too feisty too soon."

"No, really, I'm okay," Will argued. "I can make it under my own steam if you'll guide me around the furniture. The big stuff I can maneuver, but anything spindly sort of blends in."

"Was the optic nerve damaged?" Grayson asked.

"Hell, I don't know," Will snapped, then was immediately sorry. "Look, I don't even know if the bullet's still in my head, okay? Let's go ask Holly." He started for the door and tripped on the scatter rug.

Grayson caught him. "You better slow down."

"Or get a fast dog and a cane."

"No use making light of it, son. We'd best get somebody who can see about your eyes."

"My thoughts exactly. I told Holly to," he said as Grayson led him out of the bathroom.

The hallway seemed miles longer than before. Will's legs felt so wobbly, he had to accept support and lean heavily.

However, instead of walking him back to the bedroom on their left, Grayson guided him right, into the kitchen. No question, that's what the room was. The scents of bacon frying and coffee perking permeated the place.

Sunlight through the window silhouetted Holly's head and shoulders. "Brunch?" he asked, forcing a smile.

"You bet. You up to some real food now, kiddo?"

She'd never called him that before. It was a name she reserved for Eric Vinland, youngest of their team. It rankled, being called that, but Will knew it would be childish to make an issue of something that trivial. He decided to ignore it.

"Heaven must smell pretty much like this," he commented, striving for congeniality, hoping he sounded at least halfway normal. "I don't know if my stomach is ready for the menu, but my nose is having a field day."

"Park him right there, Doc," Holly said. "I've got some oatmeal with his name on it."

"Oh, Lord. Go ahead and shoot me," Will muttered as he took a chair, his feigned good humor fading fast.

"Somebody already took care of that," she quipped. "Now we have to get you well so you can shoot him back, okay? Mind Mama and eat your porridge so you'll be a big, strong boy."

She set something in front of him and began fussing over it. Adding sugar, butter and cream, he supposed. Not that he was going to eat the stuff, no matter what she did to it.

As close as she was to him, her arm brushing his shoulder, her head next to his, Will caught the familiar subtle scent of her. It jarred memories of holding her close last night, early this morning.

His appetite for food might be nil, but another appetite definitely was increasing. He needed to fight it. Rather, he ought to *keep* fighting it as he had, off and on, for a couple of years now.

Talk about denial. How the hell had he buried something like that in his subconscious?

Getting as close to death as he had must have loosened his grip. Matt would laugh about this. Matt, the wild one, the compulsive rule breaker. Wouldn't he just love this little twist of events?

Told you so! Told you so! The voice in his mind was childish, high-pitched, taunting. Matt's.

Will smiled to himself.

Had he really gone around the bend? Probably he was just delirious from hunger. He rested his head on Holly's arm as she stirred his oatmeal. "I dreamed about your omelettes. Nobody makes them the way you do."

She made a rude sound he was used to. "You are *not* conning me into feeding you something else."

She lifted his hand off the table, stuck a spoon into his palm and closed his fingers around the handle, then dragged his other hand to the bowl.

"Okay, hotshot. We know your nose is working. Let's see if you can find your mouth."

In less than three hours, Holly noted a huge difference in Will. He had been up and around most of the morning. She admired his dedicated efforts to regain his strength and deal with his temporary handicap.

There was no malingering, no slamming things around in anger. She seriously doubted she would have been able to handle herself as well if the situation were reversed. But Will was Will, practical and determined as ever.

Holly couldn't help thinking how he was the antithesis of the men she had known growing up. Maybe that was the fascination he held for her. He didn't have that in-your-face attitude—a trait she admitted to having a bit of herself. But even so, Will was anything but soft. That quiet intensity of his could project a much greater menace than any loud posturing or fist waving could ever do.

She had never heard him raise his voice in anger.

That tightening of his strong, square jaw and slight narrowing of the eyes, combined with a calmly voiced promise of consequences, was enough to do the trick.

Another thing about Will was that he listened, really heard what a person had to say. And he usually spoke little, just enough to get his point across. The result was that he held everyone's attention when he did speak.

That reserve of his always made her want to shake him up and see what would happen when he really got ruffled.

It was early afternoon when he appeared at the door to her room.

"Hey, Will, come on in." She watched Grayson guide him over and place his hand on the back of the empty chair. "Have a seat. Jack pulled some photos he thought might match my little portrait of our perp. I'm waiting for them to download."

Grayson left them alone, and she shifted impatiently in the computer chair while she waited for the pictures to appear. Jack had formatted them for high resolution and that would take awhile.

"Well, is he there?" Will demanded, obviously as eager as she was to find out whether their shooter was in the array of possible subjects Jack had collected from various data banks. The chair beside hers squeaked as he scooted it closer. Their shoulders touched; his leg brushed hers.

Holly shifted a bit, breaking contact, though she could still feel his warmth next to her. "We'll soon know."

Jack needed more details than she had transmitted earlier after she had debriefed Will. She hoped he might have remembered something else since then.

"Describe who you saw that day," she suggested as they waited.

He sighed. "Okay, one more time. The strike team was late. The plane was loaded. We either had to disable it or put the terrorists out of commission. We counted six guys, the number we'd been notified were involved in the transport. We shot up the plane first. A firefight ensued. We took them down. Firing ceased."

"Go on," she encouraged.

He swallowed hard. "Matt and I approached the plane, verified the missiles were inside, then I called you."

He paused and looked as if he was gearing up to recount the rest.

Holly put a hand on his arm. "How long after the firing stopped were you and Matt hit?"

Will paused for a few seconds, his brow furrowed. "At least seven, maybe ten minutes. We had time to check for survivors and secure the wounded guy, look inside the plane, then call it in."

"But you had a warning."

"I saw a shadow move near the hangar. We weren't wearing night vision equipment. You know how it screws you up if there's a sudden flare. A flashlight can blind you and make you a target. Firing commenced. Matt threw himself at me and took us both to the ground. That's all I remember."

"Okay, now what did you see in the hospital? In your mind, you saw this guy coming down the hallway."

"No, it wasn't like that. I knew where he was in relation to us, I guess. I felt his intent while he was psyching himself up for the kill. Matt always said that he could grasp things like that when a subject's emotions ran high. It was just feelings, and…glimpses of what he was seeing, I think.''

Holly studied Will for a long minute. She was sort of surprised he was willingly describing his episode of extrasensory perception in as careful detail as he had the actual events at the airfield. ''What were the visuals?''

Will shrugged. ''The weapon. I got a fix on that, unless my mind's playing tricks. Some kind of plastic deal, I think. Featherweight. Weird looking. He was really proud of it, as if he'd made it himself. Almost laughing at how simple it was to get it past the detectors.''

''Excellent, Will. That's exactly what he had,'' Holly said softly, encouraging him to continue. ''Anything else? Try to remember.''

He turned inward, she could tell, concentrating hard. ''Anger. Contained fury, though. He had to kill me.''

''He was afraid you'd glimpsed his face that night,'' she guessed. ''He had to get to you before you recovered and were able to do exactly what I'm about to do right now—match his face with an identity.''

''How would he know that I hadn't already done that?'' Will asked. ''He'd have to have a contact at the hospital, or with somebody who was keeping close track of my condition.''

''Right. I'm sure that's what Eric's following up on.'' She glanced at the monitor, where the first picture had materialized. ''Here we go.''

''What did he look like?'' Will asked.

''Average height. Bushy eyebrows. I'm pretty sure the hair and mustache were fake. His shoulders sloped, sort of like a no-neck athlete, you know?''

Will sat quietly beside her as she examined the five

photos Jack had sent with his first message. "Not any one of these guys," she reported with a puff of frustration.

She opened the next e-mail, with more files attached. "Rats. This could take forever."

For a long while there was no sound other than the click of the keys and her own occasional hum of disappointment.

Then Will said, almost to himself, "If I could get something of his, something he touched… I don't know if I can read him that way, but did he drop anything?"

Holly thought for a minute. "Shell casings at the airport? He would have touched those while loading. The dart from the nurse's neck?"

Will shrugged. "I don't know. It was just a thought, something to try, but it's pretty far-fetched. Tell Jack to send what he's got, just in case. Eric's probably tried everything already, since clairvoyance is his bag. Mine is… I don't really know what mine is," he admitted with a grunt. "If it's anything at all."

"It's not like Joe's snapshot images, is it?" She shook her head before he answered. "No, that's precognitive, and so are Clay's visions, except that he has to seek them out, and then they're too symbolic to mean much until after the fact. But yours seem to be real-time telepathy."

"Added to remote viewing, apparently," he added. "Like Matt's."

"Can you read me?" Holly asked. "Try it."

He was silent for a while, then sighed. "No. Nothing. What are you thinking?"

"That we'll ask Jack for the objects, anyway. It's

certainly worth a shot,'' Holly said, and promptly fired off an e-mail to that effect.

She really should encourage Will to keep trying to get in touch with his newfound ability and explore it to the max. "If it's not too painful for you, would you tell me about Matt and how you both dealt with his perceptions?"

"He had them and I didn't. At least I never picked up on anything from other people. With Matt, I pretty much knew what he was thinking most of the time. We didn't talk about it, it just *was*."

"And you never even attempted to do what he did?"

Will shook his head. "Hell, no. He caught a lot of flack because of it when we were kids. He never denied it, though. It was part of him and he used it, just took it for granted most of the time."

"Maybe you suppressed your ability early on because people gave him such a hard time about it," Holly guessed. "That would be a natural reaction."

"Spare me the pop psychology."

"That's *my* bag, in case you never noticed. People actually pay me for it."

As usual, Will ignored her tone. "We were thoroughly analyzed by experts, believe me. Matt enjoyed confusing them. He really got into those so-called studies."

"Matt was a show-off," Holly said with a smile. "You were always the quiet one."

"*Were?*"

She patted his arm and sighed. "Yep. You realize you've discussed more personal stuff with me in the last few hours than you have in all the time I've known you? And that's a good thing, Will."

"Forced proximity, I imagine. Nothing else to do."

"No, it's more than that. Different," Holly argued. "You and I have been on secluded ops before with plenty of time and opportunity for conversation, and you hardly said anything at all about yourself."

"Maybe you never let me get a word in," he teased, then sobered a little. "I think I get what you're trying to say. Maybe I'm even reading you a little right now. You're worried I'm taking on Matt's characteristics. Trying to *be* him now that he's gone. I was his shadow for so long and now the substance of us is gone."

"No, that's wrong, Will. You're obviously not reading *my* mind but projecting your own worry. Matt was *not* the substance. You were two separate and very valuable individuals. You might have looked identical, but you were so different from each other. Maybe you don't see it that way, but I always have," Holly assured him. "We chose *you* for the Sextant team. Just you."

"Only because of the language thing."

"No, not entirely. You do have a super background in Middle Eastern languages, but Matt had Russian."

Will shrugged, looking slightly uncomfortable.

"No! Don't tell me. You subbed for him in class. Will, that was cheating!"

"No, we never switched. He…we thought about it, but that would have put him at a big disadvantage if he'd ever had to use it. I only…well, sort of tutored him."

She sat up straight and stared at him in surprise. "You speak Russian? You never listed that!"

He shrugged again. "I never formally studied it. Not in class. I might have had to justify that if I'd put it on my résumé."

"Yeah, and it would have made Matt's list of creds look even slimmer than yours, right?"

She slid her arm around his waist and laid her head on his shoulder. "Don't ever sell yourself short, Will. You were never Matt's shadow. You were his support. You were his anchor, his rudder."

Will laughed. "His sail, too? If you knew how much both of us hated boats, you'd come up with another analogy."

He rested his head against hers and patted the hand she had placed on his arm. "But I see what you're saying and I appreciate the thought. Matt would have laughed his butt off at this whole conversation."

"I bet he would. But you ought to listen to me."

"I always listen to you," he said softly. "It's one of the great joys of my life, listening to you, even when you don't make a lick of sense."

They laughed together. Holly felt his steady warmth flow through her like a balm. It amazed her how they could be together this way with nothing sexual happening at all, and yet feel empowered with the energy of it.

"You should go back to work," he said, lifting his head away from hers and disengaging. "I'm getting maudlin here. Must be the drugs." But they both knew he hadn't taken so much as an aspirin all day long.

He stood, catching his foot on the leg of the computer desk and cursing under his breath. She barely stopped herself from reaching out and giving him a hand. That fierce independence of his needed to assert itself, and she needed to help it do so more than he needed her in mom mode.

He recovered his balance and braced his hand on the edge of the desk. "If you'll excuse me, I think I'll make myself scarce for a while."

"Going out to run a few laps?" she quipped to hide her disappointment.

"Sure, why not? Need me to pick up anything while I'm out? Be sure you describe it by feel."

Holly groaned. "He made a joke! A blind joke, too! Red letter day in the life of Mr. Solemnity."

"Point me to the door," Will said with a disgusted shake of his head. "Now I'm all turned around."

"Go to your two o'clock and straight ahead," she suggested.

"Walk me into the wall and I'll trade you in on a guide dog," he warned.

"Two jokes in one day. That qualifies as a stand-up routine."

"Get to work, Holly," he ordered with a backward wave. "One of us needs to be earning our pay."

"Slave driver."

She clicked the keys, pretending to be busy as she watched him make his way to the open door.

He veered a tad off course and touched the wall, then slid his hands along it in both directions until he found the door frame.

Her fingers continued making noise on the keyboard. A tear leaked out and she quickly dashed it away.

What if his blindness became permanent? She wanted so much to hold him, to protect him, but he would never accept that. Not now. He would see any offer she made as pity.

The awful thing was, she did feel sorry for him and couldn't deny that she did. She knew how she would hate it if he, or anyone else, ever felt that way about her.

Damn, she almost wished she were the one out there

running down leads, and someone else had been assigned to watch Will's back.

She didn't really mean that, Holly admitted as soon as she thought it. She couldn't be anywhere right now but exactly where she was. Even if Jack relieved her and ordered her to go, she couldn't leave Will in anyone else's care.

With a heavy sigh and a heavier heart, she turned to the computer and began scanning faces for the features of his would-be assassin.

Chapter 4

None of the photos looked remotely like the shooter in the hospital. Holly ran them through the shredder and called Jack with the bad news. There would be others, he promised. The search had hardly begun.

Time for a break. She went to the old wardrobe and thumbed through the generous stacks of clothing bought specifically for witnesses who might arrive here without luggage.

She doffed the sweats she had put on that morning, and found herself a tank top and shorts. Then she headed for the room with the exercise equipment, hoping to sweat off some of the tension.

The sound of sliding weight cables reached her before she got there. Grayson must be working out.

Uh-oh, not Grayson. That was so not him.

The sight of Will made her freeze in the doorway. He was wearing only a pair of knit running shorts, lying on his back, gripping the bar on the pulley, straining every muscle as he slowly drew it down to his chest.

A fine sheen of perspiration coated his entire body. Every bulge of muscle shone, even the finely sculpted thighs and calves.

She jerked her gaze to his face for her own peace of mind. His features gleamed, too. Sweat beaded and rivulets ran off his forehead, leading her eye down to the flexing muscles of his neck.

Her breath had stuck in her throat, but oxygen deprivation did absolutely nothing to dull her appreciation. Man, he was something *else*.

Nope, he wasn't bad at all, she thought with a grin, noting the snake-and-anchor tattoo stretching over his biceps. She knew he had gotten it during his stint in the marines.

In belated rebellion to all that family money, he and his brother had struck out on their own the summer after their freshman year, served their three years and then returned to college, wiser, calmer and as totally independent as self-made men. Also determined to make a difference in their world. They certainly had done that.

She admired Will so much. His dedication. His courage. His incredible mind. And there was a whole lot more of him to appreciate in addition to those inner attributes.

Not that this was the first time she had seen him nearly naked. There was the episode in the bathtub. Also they swam together at the gym now and then. It was just that before they'd come here, she had been very careful not to risk more than an occasional glance.

Now she might as well indulge herself. Who was to know?

She'd seen the other guys on their team almost in the buff, as he was, but they never stopped her breath like this. She sucked in a deep draft of air and released it slowly, trying to regain her equilibrium. It was so bad of her to ogle him this way when he was lying there working out and totally unaware of it.

"What's the...matter? Can't get it...in gear, Amberson?" he taunted between grunts.

She grimaced. So he *did* know. How? "Uh, I was trying to decide on a machine. Lots of choices."

Hurriedly, she jumped on a treadmill and switched it on. "How'd you know it was me instead of our illustrious host?"

"Smelled you," he gasped as he let go of the bar. The weights clanged down. "Oops, sorry."

"You smelled me?"

He grinned as he got up. "Yeah. That sort of peachy thing you've got going on."

A slight pause followed as he felt his way over to the stationary bike, climbed on it and began pumping. *Oh, Lord, what legs.*

She looked away, glancing heavenward for help. Then he said, "But I can still detect your scent even when you aren't wearing any. Pure Holly."

"I stink?" she snapped, absolutely horrified.

He laughed. "No. It's just my finely tuned nose and your pheromones or something."

"Oh là là. Griffin's got à case on me," she said in a singsong voice, hell-bent on diluting his observation and her reaction to it with silliness, to show him she wasn't taking this seriously. "Griffin's sniffing me *out.*"

He laughed again, harder this time, slowing on the cycle. "Don't *do* that. You're wrecking my pace."

"I live to amuse. Take a break, Willie boy. You're sweating like a pig. Probably croak with an aneurism or something."

She was only half joking now. He was red in the face and nearly gasping.

So was she, but not from exertion.

Grayson came in, a veritable road map of scars and wrinkles. Holly wondered if he had once been a prime example of manhood, as Will was now.

He winked at her and she grinned back. Yeah, she imagined he had been. Still wasn't bad for his age. "Hey, handsome."

Grayson blushed and ducked his head. "You two sure are industrious. Time to call a halt, son," he ordered Will. "That's enough for today."

Will protested for only a few seconds, then wound down to a stop. He got off the cycle and held up a hand until Grayson placed it on his shoulder to lead him out.

Thinking over what Will had said about detecting her scent, Holly inhaled deeply as he passed her treadmill.

Goodness. Pure male, a bit more potent than usual, she decided with a gusty sigh.

Then other senses reengaged as she watched him leave the room. His buns looked so firm beneath that soft gray knit, she could almost feel them under her palms.

Oddly enough, she could sense he was thinking about her, too, right that minute, imagining how she looked getting sweaty and hot.

Who exactly had a case on whom? she wondered, punching up the speed on the treadmill, trying to concentrate on the burn. It was a good thing neither of them were taking this interesting little event seriously.

That she found Will wildly attractive came as no big revelation. She had even teased him and called him eye candy to his face a time or two.

That the attraction might be mutual certainly was news, and not *good* news, either. It could ruin everything they had built together.

Will couldn't believe he had admitted what he had to Holly. He figured he must have some serious brain dysfunction going on. Never mind that it was all true, a guy didn't say that kind of thing to a friend. That he recognized her scent? No, you said that to a woman you wanted to seduce. God help him if Holly had taken it that way.

Since he couldn't see, maybe his other senses were overcompensating. The problem with that reasoning was that he had always been able to detect her presence, even before the injury.

It was not only her scent. Holly had a certain essence or energy surrounding her, a force field of her own that seemed to alert him whenever she was near. A great feeling every time, but not necessarily comfortable. He'd always had to work really hard not to respond to her as a man to a woman.

Times like now, that proved entirely too great an effort. As much as she wanted and insisted on it, Will couldn't seem to view Holly as one of the guys. Today it seemed he couldn't even pretend anymore.

"She's a good-lookin' gal. Seems smart, too," Grayson said as he adjusted the shower for Will. "All this affirmative action stuff sometimes don't work out so good in actual practice, though. She any good on the job?''

"She's the best," Will assured him. "Absolutely qualified in every aspect."

"Other respects, too, I betcha," Grayson commented with a suggestive chuckle.

Anger shot through Will at the inference. "You're treading dangerous ground, Doc."

"Settle down, son. I'm too old to give you a run for your money. All I'm saying is that she looks hot as a two-dollar pistol and you are one lucky devil."

Will strove for patience. Grayson was obviously old school and didn't understand the equal roles women played in the world today. What cave had he been living in?

"Amberson's an excellent friend, a member of my team, and we work together. Believe me, Grayson, that's the full extent of my *luck*."

The old guy snorted, sounding amused. "Then I'd be guessing that's your own fault, considering the way she's been looking at you."

Now that sounded exactly like something Matt would have said. Before Will could digest that and come up with a retort, he sensed he was alone. The shower was on, ready.

Will shucked off his shorts, pulled back the shower curtain that ringed the oversize tub and got in. He fiddled with the tap until he had the water running cold.

Just what he needed, the old man's imagination fueling his own.

There had been some very strong vibes in the gym room, however. And she *had* been watching him. Her gaze had felt like a laser on his skin.

Definitely his imagination was getting out of hand here.

Will turned and faced the jets of water, shivering as the icy needles chilled him all the way down his front. He ducked under the spray and soaked his head, too, while he was at it. Maybe that would lessen the brain swelling.

As soon as Will joined Holly back in the kitchen, Mercier phoned, mainly to see whether they had settled in properly, but also to inform them that no further progress had been made on locating the missing weapons or discovering the identity of Odin.

Will kept his part of the conversation short and to the point, assuring Jack that he was feeling much stronger and had completed his earlier debriefing by Holly to the best of his ability.

"I've kept in touch with your parents," Jack told him.

"Thanks. They appreciate that, I'm sure." Will was unable to keep his tone from sounding dry.

"Your father insisted before they left. He *is* the attaché, Will. He needed to return to Italy when he did. If you want to talk to him, it's okay to call him at the embassy. The lines at both ends are secure. If you'd like to speak with your mother, we can always set up—"

"Not necessary. Tell them I'm fine."

"Are you?" Jack insisted, his voice edged with concern.

"I will be."

"How's the vision?"

"Could be better." Will didn't want to discuss that. He didn't even want to think about it. "Sorry to leave you shorthanded like this. Thank Solange for her care in the chopper, okay? And say hi to the others for me. Look, I'll turn you over to Holly now.''

She took the phone when he held it out, and began speaking to Mercier. Will only half listened.

He'd been in grave danger of getting too emotional, thinking about all that Jack, his wife and the guys had done while he was out like a light.

He had missed so much while unconscious. Lost so many days. Lost so much else. It seemed to be hitting him in increments, some larger and sharper than others. All unexpected, like pieces of shrapnel from an explosion that had changed his life irrevocably.

How could he deal with this? How could he stand it? He had to fight the urge to panic about his eyes almost every minute he was awake. And he couldn't even imagine a world without his brother in it.

''Y'know, some fresh air would help you, I bet,'' Holly was saying, her voice brisk as a cool breeze. She had finished the call, he realized, and was talking to him. ''C'mon. Let's go veg on the back porch while Grayson cooks us some supper.''

Will shook off his mood as best he could, focusing on how much he hated this god-awful passivity. He was used to taking action, making decisions for himself.

He straightened his shoulders as he stood up. ''That sounds a little too *Green Acres* for me, but okay, if you insist.''

''Shut up or I'll feed you to the pigs.'' She grabbed his hand and tugged him along. ''I'm starting to really get off on this farm stuff. Did you know there are actually four cows out there in the back? Do cows bite?''

Grayson's laughter followed them out. Will couldn't

contain his own grin. Holly was a true master when it came to distraction, and it seemed she'd go to any extreme in doing that, deliberate or not.

Holly was glad she'd encouraged Will to join her out on the porch. She needed to wind down a bit and so did he. Obviously the physical workout had helped. His color had returned to normal except for lingering shadows beneath his eyes.

He had showered after exercising, changed into clean, light gray sweats, and combed his hair. He looked good enough to devour, but she definitely wouldn't think about that.

They sat together on an old fifties-style metal glider that had seen better years. For a while they simply rocked, enjoying the quiet and the bracing nippiness in the air.

She thought about how best to get him to share a few more of those feelings he seemed determined to seal off. They had made a good start, but it looked as if she might have to start all over loosening him up every time they sat down together to talk seriously.

"You're going to have to trust me, Will, and I know you have trust issues."

"What?" he asked, appearing dumbfounded by what she'd said. "I trust you implicitly, Holly. Always have. Why in the world would you think I don't? There's no one I know that I'd rather have watching my back."

She laughed and gave him a playful poke in the ribs. "You silver-tongued devil, you always say the correct thing, don't you?"

He caught her hand and held it, as if he thought she might get up and go away. "Tell me what you meant."

"Trust is a rare commodity," she said, placing her

free hand over his. "I have problems with it myself."
She sighed. "But I'm not talking about on the job.
We're all well trained, dedicated and so forth. We
know we can depend on one another in tight situations.
But it's personal, not professional, trust that's the prob-
lem here."

"You're a good friend, the best. Of course I trust
you," he protested, sounding hurt.

"Well, that's great to hear because you need to open
up some more, Will."

"We did talk," he protested. "I spilled my guts
about Matt. What more do you want?" He folded his
arms tightly across his chest, a classic defense posture
against her verbal prodding.

"This is not about me. Talk about your parents and
get that resentment out of the way. It's eating you, isn't
it, that they popped in for Matt's funeral, then left you
there comatose, in that hospital bed, and went their
merry way. You're mad as hell about it."

It was his turn to laugh, but the sound was acrid.
"Sounds as if you are, too. They were never there for
us, Holly. I hardly know the people. They sure as heck
don't know me. We only happen to be related."

"Will, they did call while you were out of it, every
single day. And your dad did have to get back. He has
an important job, you know."

"Oh yeah, Mr. Embassy Dilettante. Entertaining
people. How critical is that?" Will threw up a hand in
a gesture of frustration and let it fall by his side.

"Sometimes very crucial, and you know it." Holly
took his fist in her hand to establish a physical link.

He made a deprecating sound with his lips. "So they
spared a few days between parties. Now they have Jack
calling them to report on me, to salve their parental

conscience. Got to do the right thing and check on the kids." He shook his head sadly. "Rather, the one kid they have left."

"Some people aren't blessed with nurturing instincts. That's a fact."

"So I should quit secretly bellyaching and get over it, huh?" he said with a wry grimace. "Okay, all done now. They are who they are and I hate it. It used to hurt and it still does. See there, I've trusted you with my deepest, darkest embarrassment."

"You were lucky to have Matt," she reminded him.

"Not so lucky now," he replied with a shrug. "I haven't had the chance to fully miss him yet, and I understand that. No doubt it will get worse before it gets better."

He squinted into the distance, as if gazing out over the hills she knew he couldn't see. His voice was quiet, his hand restless in hers.

"It's like he's around, as if I can still sense what he's thinking from time to time. Reminds me of amputees and how they say there's a phantom feeling in the missing limb. Like that," he explained. He might have been reasoning it out for himself instead of her.

After a minute or two, he shook it off and turned, his vacant gaze landing over her shoulder somewhere. "Now, how about reciprocating? Throw a little trust in my direction. What was your life like?"

"Oh, baby, you don't even want to go there. I grew up on the south side of Chicago. Mean streets."

"Made you tough, huh?" He relaxed, his elbow resting on the rust-flecked arm of the glider, his head propped on his hand. "But your mom was great, right? I liked that thing where she used to draw happy faces on your food. Great story."

His smile was so charming, Holly wanted to fall right into it and kiss him on the mouth. Instead, she focused on the memory he had stirred. "Ketchup sandwiches. Syrup on the French toast. Yeah, Mama could always make me laugh, even when things were at their worst."

"She was your greatest fan," he said, nodding. "That's how it should be."

So he remembered all those little anecdotes she had related about her mom.

"Yep, and she was the inspiration for all my high-flying plans. I was determined not to sacrifice my chances to get both of us out of that hellhole by flipping out over some local homey and a few minutes pleasure with him in an alley. Kept to myself," she said. "Studied hard."

Will raised their joined hands and smacked a kiss on her knuckles. "You certainly succeeded. It couldn't have been easy in that environment."

She got up and tugged on his hand. "Enough about that. Let's go see if supper's ready. I cede to your powers of interrogation, sir. You sure turned that conversation around backward. I was trying to help you."

He stood and drew her into a hug, his arms surrounding her, his chin resting on top of her head. They swayed together, almost a dance. "You did," he said. "You always do."

Simply that. No embellishment. No profuse thanks. That was more like the Will she knew. But he seemed easier with himself now, more in tune. And she felt… warm, even though there was a definite chill in the night air.

By the time they reached the kitchen, Will was clamoring for a steak, arguing with Doc about running him out of the exercise room that afternoon when he had barely gotten started on a workout.

His concerted effort to recover instantly didn't surprise her. She wouldn't have expected any less of him.

He seemed to have accepted Matt's death and was dealing with it, she thought.

As for the problem with his eyes, he must have convinced himself that would go away, that he could will it to happen. She hoped to God he was right.

Holly ladled up three bowls of the hearty beef stew Grayson had prepared. "Great setup you've got here," she said, complimenting him.

As custodian of the safe house, he had provided just about everything a person secreted away in protective custody could need.

Grayson said the security system was top-notch. There was a huge freezer that held enough food to feed an army, and the beds he had chosen were so comfy. Doc deserved praise.

The exterior belied the conveniences hidden within. Anyone approaching the place would see a dilapidated old Victorian in need of paint, and property that sorely needed landscaping. The house had been built out in the middle of nowhere.

A fifteen-year-old sedan with missing tires sat up on blocks in the yard. A scruffy glider with torn cushions, much like the one on the back porch, and a webbed lawn chair graced the front. Not a very welcoming homestead until you got past the entrance hall.

Holly smiled at the older man. "I understand we're the first to enjoy your hospitality."

"Yep, and it's good to have somebody else around. Gets lonesome," Grayson replied. "I hope you folks don't mind the lack of cable on the TV."

"Don't think I'll miss it that much," Will said with a deadpan expression.

Holly shared a look with Grayson as she placed Will's spoon in his hand and nudged it so that he touched the bowl in front of him. "Here you go. Stew this time."

His lips tightened a little, but otherwise, he accepted the necessary help without comment and silently began to eat.

There was tension as the meal progressed, but it wasn't unbearable.

Grayson was no conversationalist, and Will certainly wasn't talkative. Holly refused to sit there and blather on by herself.

Several times she noticed Will go very still, as if he were concentrating hard on something other than his food. She wondered if he was trying to zero in on what she or Grayson were thinking. That's exactly what she would be doing if she were him. Testing her powers.

It would be great if he could discover the limits of this new ability and put it to good use. If he did, he might not feel quite so lost, not being able to see.

Will really hated being so dependent. As willing as she was to do everything she could for him, she could understand how he felt about it.

Holly figured he would become more accepting as he got used to needing help. He had his pride, but most of the time he was more pragmatic than bullheaded.

Suddenly he went tense, straightened and put down the spoon. "He's here, Holly. The shooter's here."

Almost simultaneously, a buzzer sounded on the perimeter security panel.

Chapter 5

Grayson got up and quickly shut it off. "Prob'ly just a deer tripping the electronic fence. Happened before. But I'll go check—"

"No!" Will exclaimed, pushing to his feet. "It's him. Odin. Holly?"

She was already out of her chair. "You call in the troops, Doc. Give me the car keys first. I'm getting Will out of here now."

Grayson looked at both of them as if they were nuts. But he tossed her a key ring, then turned to the small screen that sat on the kitchen counter. "The breach is to the north," he said as he grabbed his rifle off its rack. "Moon's bright, but if anyone is coming in from there, I think you can make it to the shed without being seen. The door's constructed of balsa for a quick exit. Just drive straight on through it."

"You watch yourself, Doc," she warned him.

"I will. There's a full tank. I'll cover you if I see any movement to shoot at."

Holly grabbed her purse, put the strap over her head so that the bag lay across her body like a leather knapsack. She took Will's hand and placed it on the band. "Here, hang on to this strap and stay a little behind me, okay?"

She whispered every few seconds, warning him of the steps, and when they reached the yard, of the changes in terrain so he wouldn't stumble.

All the while, Holly held her firearm ready, scanned the moonlit landscape, alert for anything that moved.

When gunshots erupted from inside the house, she picked up speed, got Will into the shed and helped him into the passenger side of the sedan. Doc was providing the promised cover.

"Seat belt. Can you get it?"

"Got it." Will's voice sounded strained and tight with frustration.

"Hold my weapon." She nudged his hand with the Glock and he palmed it. It took her only seconds to get around to the driver's side.

"Here we go!" She cranked the engine and peeled out through the breakaway door. Accelerator to the floorboard, she sped down the weed-choked driveway to the main road.

Holly dredged up all her lessons in high-speed driving. Minutes later, they were well down the road, headed for the interstate, a distance of about fifteen miles.

"Uh-oh," she muttered when she saw lights behind them. They had gone about five miles. Ten more ahead before reaching civilization. "Company."

She leaned forward as if that would make the sedan

pick up speed, though she knew it was already giving the maximum effort. "Houston, we have a problem."

"What's he driving?" Will demanded.

"It looks like a truck or a big SUV." She glanced in the mirror again. "Damn, it's an all-terrain, whatever it is. He's cutting across that field I curved around. Trying to head us off."

"Got anything besides the Glock with you?"

"My backup .22 in my purse. Don't get any ideas," she warned. "I don't want you shooting *me*. You just hold on to the Glock and keep the safety on until I need it." She sucked in a deep breath, hoping more oxygen to the brain would give her some ideas.

The vehicle after them was close, too close. It looked as if it might intersect their path before they reached the bridge ahead.

It bounced onto the main road a hundred feet shy of the narrow crossing, plowed straight into the sedan and shoved it toward the railing of the bridge. Metal screeched. She smelled rubber. *Gas? Oh, God!*

Holly battled for control. She slammed the brake pedal to the floor, spun the steering wheel, then stomped on the accelerator, attempting a one-eighty. No go.

The larger vehicle shoved them head-on toward the concrete barrier. There was nothing she could do.

"We're going in! Hold on, Will!" she screamed, still fighting with the wheel.

Her airbag had already begun to deflate when they struck the rail. The impact slammed her forward and back again like a boneless rag doll.

The seat belt grabbed her as they plunged. She never knew when they hit the water.

* * *

Will struggled to hold on to every lesson he'd ever learned about surviving in a submerged vehicle.

"Holly?" he said softly, then louder, but got no answer. He popped the catch on his seat belt, leaned across her to release hers, then fumbled for the main switch that opened all the windows. Thank God they were still working.

The doors wouldn't budge. The faster the car went under, the safer they'd be. Water gushed in through the open windows.

He still gripped the Glock she had given him. It felt welded to his hand. He found her purse and zipped the gun inside it.

Carefully he tugged Holly's inert form from beneath the wheel to make sure she wasn't trapped there. He felt her neck and found a strong pulse.

If their pursuer began firing into the vehicle and they couldn't get out, they'd be fish in a barrel. No use for Will to fire the Glock on the chance he might get lucky and hit something. It would only alert whoever was shooting at them that they were still alive.

Holly still had the purse strap around her neck. He made certain it was secure in case they needed the gun later.

Water engulfed them swiftly. He lifted her as high as he could, feeling her face with one hand, making sure she could get air from the pocket of it trapped under the roof of the car. The door still wouldn't open. Unequal pressure. That would even out shortly.

He heard shots, rapid fire from an automatic.

Again he tried the door. The car seemed to be leaning, sinking fast. He felt for the knob that controlled the lights, and pushed it, turning them off. At least he hoped it was the right one. Activating the cigarette lighter would hardly help.

Nothing to do but wait until the pressure equalized, then get the door open. Assuming they didn't sink sideways and land on the passenger side.

With his arm around her neck, he pressed his palm over Holly's mouth and pinched her nose shut to keep her from inhaling water as it closed over their heads.

Again he tried the door. With one foot, he pushed, and felt it give slowly. They were still sinking, more rapidly now, it seemed. Periodic bursts of bullets still thunked against the vehicle.

Holly remained limp, not offering the slightest struggle to free herself of his grip on her face. He had to release her to get them out of the car.

He found her wrist and held on to it as he exited, dragging her after him until they were both free. More shots sounded, muffled thumps, but he couldn't afford to dwell on what he couldn't control.

The current was strong, sweeping him too forcefully to fight it. He grasped Holly in a rescue hold and swam with the flow, hoping it would whisk them out of range before they had to surface.

When that moment came, Will prayed he could tell which way was up.

He had no idea if the clothing he and Holly wore was light or dark, whether they would be easily spotted. The moon must be bright, since she had identified the shape of the other vehicle on the road at a distance.

He refused to think about how much water she was inhaling or whether he'd be able to save her once he got her out of the water. If he ever *did*. He strengthened his grip on her and prayed for all he was worth.

His lungs were bursting. With all his might, Will

stroked with his free arm and kicked hard, propelling them upward. He hoped.

When his head broke the surface, he gasped. Now which way? He couldn't see a damn thing. No light. Nothing at all.

He pulled Holly tight against him and lifted her head out of the water as he tried to keep them upright. The powerful current that had swept them along so swiftly had all but deserted them now.

The urge to hurry gripped him. Holly was not breathing. How long had they been under? Not more than four minutes, he figured, judging from his own lung capacity. How far had four minutes carried them?

Will realized that all the time he'd been thinking, he had been moving them along, kicking and pulling in one direction, instinctively going where the water seemed calmest. He went with that and increased his efforts. When his foot struck the river bottom, he wanted to shout.

He got both feet under him and stood, feeling his way as the water grew shallower. The litter of dead limbs and weeds near the bank impeded his progress, but he soon had Holly deposited on dry ground, face-down.

Quickly he straddled her and began pressing to force water from her lungs.

"C'mon, Holly!" He heard a gurgling sound and felt for her mouth, then touched the ground beneath it. She had expelled some. He pressed again and again on her back, moved off and flipped her over to begin mouth-to-mouth, murmuring encouragement between breaths.

"Breathe, baby, breathe!"

Just when he thought his efforts were gaining them

nothing, he heard her cough, felt her body convulse beneath him.

"Yes! C'mon, honey. Fill up those lungs!" His voice was little more than a whisper as he ran his hands over her, urging her to suck in life-giving oxygen.

He still had no inkling how far from the bridge they were or if Odin had been able to mark their progress visually. Will was sure it was Odin. Never had a doubt of that.

They needed to get out of here. "I'm working blind, Holly, and that's no damn joke. I *need* you conscious now! Come on!"

She sputtered, gagged, groaned.

He turned her to one side and rubbed her back, caressed her head, touched her everywhere, checking for injuries. "Are you hurt?"

Again she coughed, this time hard and repeatedly, even as she struggled to sit up. He moved off of her and helped, but not much. He was too weak with relief.

"W-where are w-we?" she gasped, shivering violently.

Will lay sideways on the ground, exhausted, shaking. "You're asking *me?*"

He heard her scuffling around, checking out their surroundings. Heard also the zipper on her purse and the click of her weapon. "I can barely see the bridge from here," she told him, her voice quavery and still a little breathless. "At least I think it's the bridge."

For the life of him, he couldn't get up. He just lay there, spent and thankful. Holly was alive. Right now that was all that counted.

"Thanks, Will," she whispered. "I owe you one."

He smiled to himself. She sure did. He was not above patting himself on the back when he did good,

and saving Holly was probably the best thing he had
ever accomplished in his life. There was that old belief
that if you saved someone's life, he or she belonged to
you from that day on.

Fat chance that would ever happen, but it sure was
a nice fantasy to play with.

"Do you *mind?*" she said, obviously exasperated
with him for some reason. Maybe the goofy smile on
his face?

"We need to find some real cover," she said, taking
his arm. "We're too exposed where we are. Can you
get up?"

Had he said anything out loud?

No matter. He was halfway to his feet when something other than their own rustling movements and the
sloshing of water against the nearby bank broke the
stillness of the night.

He yanked her to the ground. "Shh! Hear that?"

"The drone of a motor! He's coming after us."

"Is it light enough to see much?" Will demanded.

"There's a moon, but it's not too bright. You think
he saw us swim out?"

"He must have. Or maybe he just saw us surface.
From the sound of it, he's moving at a crawl, headed
this way."

"Looking for us," she added.

"What's the terrain like?"

Holly cleared her throat and coughed again. He felt
her stir, guessed she had pushed herself up again to
look around. "Tall weeds, but not tall or dense enough
to hide us if he passes near the bank. It rises up from
where we are, four feet or so at maybe a twenty or
thirty degree angle to what must be a road. Woods on
the other side."

"How far away?"

"I guess around sixty, seventy feet. No way we can get there without his spotting us as we cross the road."

"Any cover over here?"

There was a slight pause, then she moved again, rustling around. "A fallen tree that's half in the water. Looks about three feet in diameter. We could lie behind that." She took his hand and tugged.

"No," he argued, halting her. "Too obvious. We're not exactly camouflaged, are we?"

"I'm wearing dark sweats, but yours are light gray."

"Damn." He thought for a minute. "Okay. Back in the water. I'll go first. You slide backward, take a minute to fluff up the weeds we mashed down. Then we hug the bank and work back upstream. When he gets parallel to us, we can submerge if we need to."

"He's getting closer. Let's do it."

Will crawled backward and slipped into the waist-high water, crouching so that only his head broke the surface. He grabbed a handful of cattails and clung to them like a lifeline until Holly joined him.

He barely heard the slosh, then her hand covered his, removing it from the weeds he was clutching and placing it on her chest. He spread his palm flat, feeling the rapid rise and fall of her generous breasts.

She was still wearing her purse, the strap crossing her body like a bandolier. He curled his fingers around it and held on so they wouldn't get separated.

He listened intently as they propelled themselves upstream, determined to work his other four senses to the max, since his sight was useless.

A sudden silence halted him. He squeezed Holly's arm with his free hand.

"Here. Move backward," she whispered, giving him a firm shove.

Will let her guide him until his back was forced against a muddy surface, water lapping at his chin. Her body pressed into his, covering him, her hands anchoring them to the bank by whatever she had grabbed on either side of him.

He felt her lips brush his ear, her words a mere breath of sound, her scent familiar and precious in the total darkness.

"The bank's undercut a little here," she was saying. "We should be safe."

"Even if he strafes the bank?" Will whispered, remembering the shots from the bridge.

"Let's hope." She tensed when they heard a car door shut, and voices. There were more than one of them.

Will and Holly clung silently, hardly daring to breathe, alert to the swish of footsteps through the tall grass.

The sudden bark of an automatic made them both jump. Another spate of bullets rent the night. And another. Close. *Too* close.

Will pulled Holly tighter against him, wishing he could reverse their positions and shelter her. It was unnatural that she should be between him and the threat, but his light clothing would glow like a beacon.

Suddenly a violent volley of evil energy hit him like a blow to the gut. Frustration. Fear. Urgency. Vile curses so vivid they might have been screamed out loud. But he knew they were silent, roiling inside the mind of the man who wielded that weapon. *Odin.*

The firing stopped. Will couldn't hear anything other than the ringing in his ears. He knew Odin was still standing on the bank, not directly above them, but way too close for comfort.

Will pressed his lips to Holly's temple and held her, his fingers memorizing the toned muscles of her back. She had her weapon in her hand, he knew. Ready to defend them as best she could, even though she was seriously outgunned.

The echoes of the shots dwindled, and again he could hear the slosh of waves against their bodies and the bank, the rustle of grass above the undercut bank where he and Holly huddled. Then he heard voices again. No, Odin was not alone.

"Are you sure you saw them come up over here, sir? I didn't see anything." The high-pitched tone could have belonged to a woman, but Will didn't think it did. He filed the supposition away to examine later.

"I think so, but it could've been my eyes playing tricks. You can hardly see this spot from the bridge, even with the scope, but it's the most likely spot for them to have climbed out if they didn't drown."

Will detected a slight Southern accent in the deeper voice, a distinctive nasal intonation. Had he heard it before? Something about it seemed familiar.

"You'll have to handle this. Can you do that?" Deep Voice asked. "I'm dropping you in Raleigh. Pick up a car and head back here at first light. Look for any sign they made it out. If they did, call immediately and I'll pinpoint their next location for you. I want them both dead, you hear? The security will be beefed up next time and it won't be easy."

"I'll take care of it," the other one assured him.

"You'd better. I have to get those missiles to Turkel at Hartsfield by the day before Thanksgiving. Timing's crucial if we want to get paid."

More rustling, then the silence stretched out.

Had they given up?

Finally a car door slammed, a motor caught and revved. Will could hear the tires digging ruts in dirt, slinging rocks, as the heavy vehicle sped away.

Holly heaved out a gasp and burrowed her head against Will's neck. "Thank God they're gone," she whispered, as if still in danger of being overheard.

Will said nothing. He was too busy thinking, trying to remember if he had ever heard the name Turkel before and if so, in what context. And where the hell was Hartsfield? For a few long minutes, he and Holly remained where they were.

Then she spoke out loud. "I guess we can ditch our fins now. You hypothermic yet?"

The water was cold, but not unbearable. Will felt a moment's regret when Holly moved away from him and placed his hand on her purse strap again. She led the way back downstream to a spot where they could climb out easily.

Exhausted beyond belief, Will levered himself onto the grassy bank and collapsed. He heard her moving around, unzipping her purse.

"My cellphone's waterlogged, but looks like it's working. I'm sending an S.O.S," Holly told him succinctly.

"Jack will need to run that name and place. Did you catch it all?"

"Yep. Turkel and Hartsfield. Any ideas?" she asked.

"I'm still thinking," Will told her.

Odin, or whatever his real name was, would be long gone by now, intent on his other business. He was on a deadline to deliver the missiles.

Why the rush? Why Thanksgiving instead of an actual date? Wasn't hard to guess. Threat levels went up during holidays, for good reason. Planes were crowded. Turkel, whoever *he* was, planned to use those weapons.

Will listened as Holly repeated word for word to Mercier the conversation they'd overheard. The phone beeped as she ended the call.

She remained quiet for a minute, then asked, "So why Thanksgiving? You think there's an attack planned to coordinate with that date?"

"Sounds like."

"Oh, Lord, and within our boundaries, too, I bet, since that's our holiday," she said. "Which means we can't take our time on this. That's what? Five, six days away."

Frustrated as he had ever been, Will pressed his fingers to his eyes and cursed under his breath. What could he do in the shape he was in?

"We have to let Jack and the others handle this one, Will," she said gently, brushing a hand over his head as if he were a child in need of comfort.

He pulled away, liking her touch too much, while at the same time resenting her pity, if that was the reason for her touch.

"One way or another, I'm going to be in on this, Holly. I'm not too proud to demand your help. You owe me."

"I do and I always pay back favors," she assured him. "After we're picked up, we'll figure out what to do next. I'll swing what weight I can with Jack and see if he'll let us have a hand in things."

"I'm holding you to that."

He heard her soft sigh. "By the way, I really do appreciate the tow out of the river. And the mouth-to-mouth."

"Any time." He rolled to his back and reached out toward the sound of her voice. "Nice mouth it is, too."

"Ooh, Griffin's kissing up. He must feel better." She grasped his hand and put it to her face. "Seriously, though, I would still be down there in that car if it weren't for you. Thanks."

"Don't mention it." Then he forced a smile into his voice. "Just act on it. You're going to be my eyes until we get Odin and those missiles where they need to be."

"You're not up to this, Will. You know that."

"I will be," he promised. "When the time comes, I'll be ready."

"Well, so far we've always worked pretty good together." Her voice sounded odd, its cheerfulness as fake as his. God, what he wouldn't give to see her face. He caressed it, feeling a warm wetness on her cheeks that he knew was not river water.

Without warning, she lay down and snuggled close beside him, embracing him fiercely as she let go a little sniffle. It was just one, but he still couldn't believe it. She didn't cry. She never cried.

Should he tease her out of this display of emotion or what? That's what he would have done before.

Now he just held her, sliding his hands over her dripping clothes, pressing his mouth to her neck, glorying in the fact that she was alive to cry, to laugh. To kiss.

He found her mouth with his, at first just a press of lips. Then he tasted her, encouraging her to open herself to him just a little. Then more fully.

A second later, she threw herself into the kiss with an abandon that proved contagious.

God, she was so sweet, lush, passionate, everything

he could have dreamed of or wished for. Exactly what he *had* dreamed of and wished for.

There was no doubt that she was affected by *this* kiss. He would never have admitted it before today, but he had wanted to kiss her this way since the day they'd first met.

to reach more attention to her subject and request what
    blood the year I must retreat and

Everyone as whole, figure speak "Good bye," he
    stale. He didn't even have a friend if chose away
    her house marry which he's to come come over a case
    so you fit ready

Chapter 6

Holly was the first to pull away. "Will?" She sounded unsteady, uncertain, unlike his Holly, who never met a situation she couldn't handle.

Will realized things were getting a little too deep for him, too. This couldn't go beyond the kiss. He had nothing to offer Holly. At least not long term, and she wasn't the type for short-term attachments.

"I don't know what that was all about, but this'll never work and we both know why," he said with a rough sigh.

"Hey, who asked you to make anything *work?* It was just a kiss," she snapped. "Get over it."

It wouldn't do to make too much of it. No reason she should know how kissing her affected him. He would get over it, just as she said. Right now. *Play it off.*

He gently pinched her cheek, tugging a little. "Okay. Now we're even on the mouth-to-mouth. See if you can drag me to my feet and lead me in the right direction. We might as well wait for pickup at the bridge.''

Cool night air replaced the warmth of her body. Her grip was strong as she tugged him to a standing position. His legs nearly buckled, but he managed to brace his knees and hold steady until he got his balance.

She released one of his hands and led him with the other up the bank and along the edge of the dirt road. He passed the time counting steps, using the tedious exercise to dull the pain in his head and in the muscles of the arm he had locked around her in the river.

It seemed they walked forever, silent, each lost in thought. He had no clue what she was thinking. He could only hope she was just as clueless about what occupied his mind.

He wanted her. Badly. Here and now. The physical attraction between them loomed powerful and heady. Subduing it took a lot of mental and physical energy. Both commodities were in very short supply at the moment.

Maybe it was his dependence on her, plus her natural instinct to nurture and protect, that threatened his good sense. If they started anything physical right now, it would be embarrassing for both of them when the danger was over and things returned to normal. The job would get in the way.

He simply could *not* follow through, even if she were willing. The whole deal would destroy their friendship and have an adverse effect on their team.

''You're absolutely right, Will. There are just too many pitfalls to getting involved. We've both seen what happens,'' she said as they trudged along, their shoes squishing with every step.

''Who was he? Fellow agent?''

"None of your business. It always comes down to a hard choice, not one I want to have to make again."

"Hazard of the occupation," he agreed. "Even with civilians, it blows up in your face."

"Haven't tried that yet, but it stands to reason."

How many times had he answered a call, leaving a woman in the middle of the night, unable to explain where he had to go, what he had to do, when he would return to pick up where they'd left off?

And when he did return, how many had been there waiting? None. So Holly had been burned, too.

He couldn't promise he would never give her an ultimatum. He had discovered tonight that he'd do damn near anything to keep her alive.

Better to ignore the heated kiss, forget the flare of desire, the almost overpowering need. Better to pretend nothing existed between them and make sure that nothing further occurred.

He walked on, mulling it over. The kiss had affected her as much as it had him. He didn't need clairvoyance to know that. Maybe it was only the result of sheer relief at being alive, he told himself, not buying the rationalization for a second even as he made it up.

Holly braced herself when Will stumbled, grasping her arm to keep from falling. She urged him off the road. "Sit down here and lean back against this tree."

"I just need a minute to rest. I'll be fine."

"Sure, no problem."

He said nothing as Holly took his wrist and checked his pulse. His skin felt cold, clammy.

What if he lapsed back into that coma? He drew in a particularly deep breath and let it out slowly, willing his body to respond to the extra oxygen. He flexed his shoulders and stretched his legs out straight.

God, he was so tired, when a little more than a week ago he would have just been working up a good sweat.

Holly went into nurse mode, feeling his face like a mother testing for fever. He could sense her frustration, her worry. ''God only knows how long you went without breathing! Or how much exertion it took to get me out of that car, hang on to me, then drag me up on the bank.''

''Get a grip, Holly,'' he huffed. ''I'm not six years old and I'm not about to expire on you, okay? I'm just tired.'' He grasped the hand that cradled his face and tugged it away. ''Now stop fussing and tell me what you see.''

She went still and he heard her clear her throat. ''Tall pines block out most of the moonlight. I can barely see anything. Wild animals still roam these parts, I bet. It's wilderness, not my kind of place. Maybe bears, cougars, wild dogs.''

''You don't sound all that scared,'' he teased.

''Are you kidding? I'd go hunting if we had time to cook the game.''

He laughed as she moved closer, the length of her arm resting against his.

But it wasn't enough. Their clothing was soaked. He was cold and she was, too.

''I think it's too risky to build a fire, don't you?'' she asked.

''Odin's buddy shouldn't be back until morning if he follows orders, but let's not take any chances.''

''That's what I thought, too. Body heat, then? Can we handle that?''

His laugh was short and wry and his only answer.

He wasn't altogether sure he could, but he was determined to do his best.

She wiggled around as if looking for something. He heard the zipper on her purse again. "I've got a roll of Lifesavers. Here, eat some of these," she ordered, pushing a couple between his lips.

He grunted his thanks and dutifully crunched the candies. Hopefully, he'd perk up a little when the sugar hit his system. She gave him more. Strange, sitting here in the woods, soaking wet, being hand-fed candy.

When he'd eaten what seemed like the entire roll, she began piling pine straw and leaves all around and on top of him to insulate him against the chill of the night.

"Hope we don't get chiggers," he muttered.

"Chiggers? What's that? Is it like the shivers?"

He didn't want to explain for a number of reasons, most of all because he didn't really want to walk anymore right then. "Something like that."

"We'll be warm enough, I think."

No doubt. Will resigned himself to it.

She snuggled full length against his side, her arms around his body, and shared what warmth she had. "This is about the extent of my survival skills in a situation like this," she said. "Sorry."

"Perfect," he mumbled as he cuddled her close, holding her as if they were lovers. "No complaints at all. And no reason to feel uneasy with this, Holly. We're just being sensible, keeping each other warm this way."

"Right. Nothing else we can do. I'm good with it."

Better than good, he thought. Damn great. He knew she'd do exactly the same thing for any of the other agents on the team. But he sure didn't want to think about her heating up this way with Joe, Clay, Jack or Eric the kid.

Her arms tightened around him when he shifted against her, fitting his length to hers as if they were made to go together.

Nobody under this tree was going to take a nap anytime soon, but they *were* warming up really fast.

Will closed his eyes and prayed for the willpower not to enjoy this too much and not to touch her the way he wanted to. This was business. That was all.

Odin stopped for gas just outside Roanoke. As he pumped fuel into the tank of the camper-covered truck, he questioned his priorities.

Maybe he should have stayed and searched harder for Will Griffin and the woman. They would be harder to get the next time, if there had to be one. Then it could be too late.

There hadn't been time to make certain both Griffins were dead at the airfield. The place would have been crawling with agents in a matter of minutes. He had cut it too close.

Maybe Griffin would never be able to identify him, but leaving him alive was too great a chance to take. That female agent, Amberson, sure had a good look in the hospital, he knew that much. Even with the disguise, she might recognize him later with his face all over the news. She was trained to do that.

Odin was almost sure they had drowned. That current was too swift for a man who had been bedridden for days to battle. The woman didn't look strong enough, either.

It could be days before the bodies turned up and proved him right. He didn't have days. If they had survived that plunge into the river, Odin knew he would just have to trust Pete to take care of it. Pete was loyal as could be and fully committed. He wasn't all that smart, but he always followed orders.

The missiles had to be delivered before the holiday. The idea of their being used here in the States troubled him, but in the long run, he knew it would double security after it happened and save many more lives than would be lost.

In times of terror, people wanted a man experienced in military matters to be in charge. He had twenty years of that, plus a distinguished appearance that would appeal to the public. His position was perfect for that.

Collateral damage was acceptable in times of war, and this *was* war. He was waging it himself. He could control when and where these weapons were used, and make certain that use didn't get out of hand. It would prove a helluva wake-up call for the powers that be.

There would also be a seriously dedicated effort to recover those thousands of SAMs now squirreled away by various groups around the country bent on destruction of the government.

Yes, this was a very necessary evil. He must make everyone aware. And then he must assume a position of responsibility to prevent further disasters. It was his duty.

Killing the terrorists after the fact would solidify his status as hero. He was the ultimate patriot. It was time he had the recognition to go with it.

He replaced the nozzle in the pump and went inside to pay for the gas.

"Well, would you look at that? It's *Survivors, Roanoke River!*" a voice crooned. "They'll have to split the million, folks."

Holly woke with a sudden jerk and bolted upright, her gun hand empty. Bright light from a battery-powered lantern lit up the little campsite.

Eric Vinland threw back his head and hooted. "You should see your face!" He waggled her nine millimeter in the air.

"I'll smash yours flat for you, you little creep!"

"*Little?* Me?" he gasped with totally fake outrage. "Where?"

"Where it counts," Holly snapped, blinking against the light.

Eric Vinland was six feet tall and in no way small, even where it counted, but verbal jabs were about all she could get him with. During the months the team had worked together, and in free time spent at the gym, she had never seen anyone, friend or foe, land a physical blow on him.

He held his hands out in a gesture of surrender and returned her weapon. "Peace, O Tawny Goddess. I bring offerings of chocolate." He reached in his pocket, then tossed a Snickers bar into her lap.

He leaned over and nudged Will's hand with another one. "Hey, Will. Does she look this ragged every morning?"

"Beats me," Will muttered.

Holly sprang to her feet, leaves flying every which way. She impatiently raked one off her face. "What time is it? Where's Jack?"

"Close to 2:00 a.m. Jack's busy trying to track down our quarry. He sent me to spirit you two out of danger and hide you again."

"How's Grayson?" Will asked. "Was he injured?"

"No, he's fine," Eric answered. "He reported what

happened back at the house. The place is compromised now, of course, and can't be used any longer. He'll be sent somewhere else.''

"Any leads yet on who Odin might be?" Will asked.

"He's an insider or knows someone in the business very well," Eric said. "Otherwise he could never have located you either at the hospital or at the safe house. That last took some doing. It might be what trips him up.''

Holly took Will's hands to help him stand. He slid his arm around her shoulders in what felt like a proprietary move.

Eric smiled suggestively at them and waggled his eyebrows. "Yes, there's no doubt about it," he continued. "The only good thing is that Odin's probably not aware of all we know. Not yet, anyway. Jack's working on that name you gave him. Turkel, wasn't it? And he's convinced Hartsfield refers to the airport in Atlanta.''

Will nodded. "That feels right and makes sense. Let's head south.''

"No way, buddy. I've got my orders. You and Holly are supposed to stay out of the picture entirely. How does yours work?''

"What?''

"Your reading him," Eric demanded, referring to the psychic connection.

"There wasn't any *reading* to it this time, not the way you mean. We actually overheard him talking. In the hospital and at the safe house, I sensed him approaching. I don't know how or why that worked the way it did, or if it ever will again. I do think maybe I felt fear on his part, anger and definitely urgency.''

Eric sighed. "Yes, well, you blew his last deal and then had the effrontery not to die after he shot you. There was a reason for his anger. He knows Holly saw his face and that you might have, too, at the airfield. That would make him afraid, I guess. But why urgency? Afraid he'll lose his customer for the missiles?"

"What he said indicated that," Will muttered. "Do you think maybe we know this guy?"

Holly was shaking her head already. "Not me. Never seen him before that night in the hospital." She thought about it for a minute. "And if you knew him, Will, he would figure you'd have blown the whistle on him as soon as you came out of the coma, right? If so, why did he wait days before the attempt to kill you?"

"Maybe it took him that long to discover where I was?" Will asked.

Eric seemed lost in thought for a minute. "Just about every operative in the agencies involved in the op would have heard you were comatose after the shooting. But I'll bet our boy was keeping closer tabs on you than that. Maybe this is someone you don't know, Will. At least not yet. However, if he let you live, you might have been able to identify him once you recovered and started working on it."

"As good a theory as any," Will agreed. "But there was a nagging sense of familiarity."

"Maybe his buddy will blab. I'm planning to be back here at dawn to liven up *his* day when he comes looking for you. We'll see how loud he squeals." Eric shook his finger at them. "But you, my friends, are officially out of the picture except for providing reports on what's already happened."

Holly objected, just as she had promised. "We're in

on it, Eric, so get used to it. Either we decide among us how we handle this or we call Jack for further orders.''

Eric smiled. "No. You have your orders. Just lie low until we catch him. I'll find you a good place."

Will nodded. "In Atlanta. I say we go with Jack's supposition about Hartsfield. I don't know how close I have to be to this guy to pick up his mental pixie dust, or even if I can do it again, but there's only one way to find out. We can at least hang out in his general vicinity and see what happens."

Eric frowned. "You're going to do this anyway, aren't you?"

Holly nodded and smiled. She knew she should object right along with Eric on the grounds that Will was not in any condition to participate, but she knew how much he needed to. How could she deny him that? Besides, he might provide their only possibility of finding Odin. She could keep Will safe.

"Okay, let's go," Eric said finally. "Nobody said I couldn't set you up with a place there, but you'd better keep a very low profile, and I mean it."

Holly squeezed Will's hand and gave it a victory shake. She hadn't even realized until then that she was holding it.

"What kind of transportation we got, kiddo?" she asked Eric.

"Harley-Davidson," Eric answered, straight-faced.

"You had *better* be joking." She followed him to the road, Will right behind her, his hand grasping her shoulder. "It would be just like you to show up on a stupid motorcycle."

But he hadn't. A few minutes later, they climbed into

a Jeep Cherokee and were on their way. Will settled in the back and Holly took the front passenger side.

Eric drove and did it the way he did everything, expertly, with little effort expended. He might appear casual about this, but excitement was rolling off him in waves.

Will was quiet, surely busy analyzing the facts, putting the puzzle pieces in place. You could almost hear the wheels turning in his head.

Holly couldn't help comparing the two men. Will always worked methodically, giving serious attention to detail and leaving very little to chance. He analyzed everything and was damn good at constructing clues out of next to nothing, putting them together and coming up with solutions.

Eric, on the other hand, seemed totally dependent on his instincts. It was almost as if he would welcome a surprise if one ever occurred, so he could use his psychic gifts.

Holly knew she struck a happy medium between the two, not as blasé as Eric, not as by-the-books as Will. Together, the three of them should be able to handle whatever came along. At least until they assessed how things stood and called in the rest of the team.

Once they located Odin, they would need all the backup they could get. Jack was going to have their hides as it was for expanding their orders, so they had to be successful.

As far as Eric was concerned, she wanted the situation made perfectly clear. She was running this phase and would take the heat for overstepping when it was all over. She didn't want Will or Eric to catch any grief over it.

"Okay, Wunderkind. This is my operation, my idea,

agreed?'' She reached over and poked his arm hard, nodding at him to insure his compliance.

Eric threw her a smile, didn't even hesitate. ''You call the shots.''

''And Will is second in command,'' Holly told him. ''You, little buddy, will be our gopher.'' She would insist she had coerced him into cooperating if Jack wanted to discipline them after it was over.

''Errand boy? That's bull. I'm in this up to my neck, little mama.''

Will spoke up from the back seat. ''Do you feel we've adopted the wrong child, Holly?''

''Yeah. Let's send him out for a loaf of bread and move before he gets back.'' She'd do it, too. They could ditch him and he knew it. Holly knew that was the only reason he had agreed for them to go to Atlanta.

''All right, all right,'' Eric grumbled. ''I'll be your flunky. Let me know when I can fetch something for you.''

''Odin's pal would be a good start.''

''Yeah, I hope that works out, but you know he won't go down easy. Wouldn't you choose a blaze of glory rather than face a terrorist charge? I'll probably have to kill him.''

''Take him alive if you can,'' Will advised.

''When you get to Atlanta, find a doctor for Will,'' Holly said. ''Can you handle that?''

''Can do. I'll even throw in a pretty nurse.''

Holly frowned at that, then quickly switched her jealous mind to business matters.

Eric laughed at her, so she knew she hadn't been quite quick enough to keep her thoughts to herself. She glanced back at Will, who was wearing a bland look of innocence.

* * *

Holly and Will kept Eric's Jeep while he scrounged another vehicle to go back to the river to wait for Odin's sidekick.

They had agreed it would be unwise to fly commercial, since Will had no identification. Requesting his ID would alert Jack. Also, putting their names on a computerized passenger list might alert someone a whole lot more dangerous to them than an irate boss.

They considered, then discarded the idea of hiring a private plane or a chopper. That expense would have to be approved through channels. It would be, immediately. However, the fewer people who knew their whereabouts and mode of transportation, the better.

After leaving Eric with his new wheels, Holly headed for the nearest hotel, a modest chain near the interstate. "First order of business is to get us dry," she told Will. "Then you need to sleep in a real bed."

"We can make Atlanta in six or seven hours," he argued.

"It's better if we wait. Let's stick around and see how things work out with Eric's little venture in the morning."

Will looked doubtful.

She continued. "We might even get an ID on Odin out of that. The bastard sure would be a lot easier to find if we had a name. Then Eric needs to get to Atlanta and find us a place to stay."

"I just want to get on with this," Will muttered. "The bomb's ticking, Holly. Who knows what they're planning for Thanksgiving?"

She shook her head, a little exasperated. "We don't know for sure they're planning anything. Maybe he just agreed to deliver them by that time."

"You know better, Holly. There are God knows how

many of those missiles floating around in the Middle East. Here, they're harder to come by, but they're still too plentiful in anybody's book. Where's the profit in stealing a small cache like this to sell? The whole lot would have brought peanuts if split that many ways. That was too much risk for too little gain. No, I think there are plans to use them.''

He was right. ''Whatever they plan, Thanksgiving's less than a week away and you can bet every agency will be on this by now. We can afford to slow down and regroup a little here. You should be rested when we get to the area. If you're goofy from exhaustion, how are you gonna hone in on Odin?''

Will shrugged, but she could see it cost him to go along with her delay.

She understood his impatience, his need to see justice done for his brother and, even more crucial, to prevent what might very well be a national catastrophe.

The thought of those Stingers aimed at planes full of holiday travelers made her sick. But everything she had told Will was true. He couldn't operate in any capacity if he was zombielike with fatigue.

She parked at the motel office and registered them for a double with two beds.

Once they were inside the room, she pushed Will into the bathroom and ordered him to strip and shower.

''Stop treating me like a child, Holly,'' he warned. ''I have just about had it with that!''

She supposed she had been a little overbearing. Usually he put up with her bossiness, even seemed amused by it, but right now he looked as if he had reached his limit. ''Okay, but I have to wait on you to get through in here. Unless you want company in this shower, get on with it.''

Just saying that sent a ripple of heat through her and shot her imagination into overdrive.

He must be experiencing a similar feeling, she realized when he turned toward her. He grabbed the tail of his sweatshirt and stripped it off over his head, then reached for the waistband of his pants, as if anticipating just what she had suggested.

Holly forced her gaze away from his bare chest, quickly turned on the water, adjusted the tap and scooted past him out of the room. One thing she absolutely did not need was to see Will naked again.

She pulled off her own damp clothes, reveling in the warmth of the room as she switched on the television to kill time while she waited. Anything to distract her thoughts from Will. She curled up on the bed, staring at the television without really seeing it.

Will Griffin was a damn fine looking man, that was all. Any woman would get a little steamed up at the sight of him. Added to that was the very compelling urge to temporarily shift her focus and his away from the problem with Odin and the Stingers, and concentrate on something life-affirming instead of something potentially deadly.

Natural responses aside, however, her attraction to him seemed harder to control. It was almost as if she'd had it bottled and stoppered inside her since the day they'd met, and now it had broken free. She didn't quite know how to get it contained again.

If only he could see and do everything for himself, they could have taken separate rooms. Too late now.

Will exited the bathroom wearing only a towel. He rubbed his hair briskly with another one. "All yours," he said, squinting at the circle of light he knew must be the lamp between the beds. Her shadow moved toward him, then to one side, and disappeared.

"Careful how you throw that offer around. A girl could misunderstand." Her laugh sounded a little strained, the teasing forced. "Go to bed, Will." Her voice came from behind him. "Be asleep when I come out of here." The door shut with a firm click.

He wanted to shake her. She was probably the bossiest woman alive. Getting bent out of shape about that served no purpose. It had never bothered him before. He and the other guys just took it for granted, enjoyed it, often joked about it.

Holly worried about them. No woman had ever cared enough to order him to do what was good for him. Certainly not his mother. Even his teachers had let him do pretty much as he pleased. He guessed his being dependent on Holly for the simplest things right now made him too sensitive.

Even knowing that, he couldn't stifle his need to assert himself and throw off the role of patient. That felt ungrateful. She'd probably see it as petty. Hell, even he saw it that way.

He ran a hand through his hair, backed up to the bed and sat down. If he had any sense left, he would do exactly as she'd said—crawl between the covers and go to sleep. Avoid temptation.

If she came out of that bathroom and approached him, he was more than liable to do something really unproductive, like kiss her again.

His motive for doing that would be suspect to say the least, even to himself. Comfort, control or desire? Even he couldn't pinpoint why he wanted to do it.

He knew what the immediate goal was, of course, but why, exactly, would he even think about jeopardizing their solid-gold working relationship? She joked around with all the guys and they joked back. Not one member of the team, least of all Holly, took the banter seriously.

The door opening alerted him that he had sat there thinking for entirely too long. Nothing for it now but to have it out in the open.

"Holly," he said firmly. "We need to talk."

"Oh, shoot. Last time some guy said that to me, he was about to dump me and take my dog."

Will patted the bed. "Sit down and stop fooling around."

"Now that's wishful thinking, my man. You want me to fool around, it will cost you a fully loaded pizza and a beer. I'm no cheap date."

"Cut it *out*, Holly!" he snapped, his patience gone.

She sighed loud and long. He felt the bed bounce as she plopped down heavily, out of his reach. Not that he had any intention of reaching for her.

He cleared his throat. "We need to get something straight."

"No sex," she said, sounding woebegone. She moved closer, between him and the light.

"Holly…"

"I know, I know, you can hardly restrain yourself. But you know Vinland would whip your ass if you—"

Will gauged where her arm would be and grasped it. She yelped a little, surprised, when he pulled her close and kissed her.

He only meant to shut her up, but her mouth welcomed his, warm, wet, delicious. He deepened the kiss, his mind drugged with the sheer power of what she made him feel.

Chapter 7

She should pull away now, Will thought dimly. He couldn't. Instead, she writhed closer, pressing against him.

Next thing he knew, they were lying down, a tangle of bare skin and damp towels. Damn little of the towels.

Her hands clutched his back, her long nails delicately scoring, sending frissons of pure lust rocketing from surface to core. He slid his own hands between their bodies, cradling her breasts, swallowing her murmur of encouragement.

Her legs moved around his hips in blatant invitation. Will had fitted himself to her, ready to make it real, when a sudden jolt of reason stopped him.

"Can't," he gasped against her seeking mouth. "We…can't do this."

"No," she moaned—whether in agreement or protest, he couldn't tell.

Even so, he forced himself to lift off of her and roll to his back. He slung an arm over his eyes and groaned.

For several minutes, they lay there side by side, touching shoulder to knee, all but hyperventilating.

When he had himself halfway under control, he risked an explanation. "No protection." His voice sounded strangled, strange to his ears. "Besides…"

"Yeah, I know. Thanks," she rasped. He heard her take a deep breath and expel it slowly.

"You're not welcome," he said, rolling his head from side to side. "Not at all."

"Let's not do this again, okay?" she whispered in a small voice.

Will nodded, unable to promise out loud. He stared at the light, trying to fix his attention anywhere rather than on her. Never in his life had he wanted anything so badly as he wanted Holly. But he would not risk a pregnancy when she was so devoted to her career. He was surprised that she would. Maybe she was on the pill. "Are you…taking anything?"

"No," she said, a woeful sound if he'd ever heard one. That made him feel a little better, that she was as disappointed as he was.

Again they fell silent until the program on the television changed. A lone, wailing saxophone cut through the stillness of the night, the music promising something sensual and suggestive. Holly cursed under her breath, wriggled off the bed and turned off the set.

She didn't return to his bed. Instead, he heard the rustle of covers on the other one. A few seconds later, the light snapped off and there was only darkness. Solitude. Regret.

They didn't even risk saying good-night. Talking

their way around this was not going to work, anyway. The only thing left to do was try to ignore it.

Holly slept until 9 a.m. when Eric's phone call woke her up. He'd had no success. Morning had dawned cold and dreary. She donned her clothes, which she had spread out to dry before her shower. She tossed Will's on the chair beside the bed when she returned to the room.

He still slept. She could hardly see him in the meager daylight that sifted around the edges of the heavy drapes.

How was she going to handle this? Pretend it had never happened. No use beating themselves up over what almost took place here. Almost didn't count. Not unless you let it. Okay, she would wake him up and see.

"Rise and shine, sleeping beauty," she growled.

It was time they got out of this motel room before they went crazy again, she thought with a roll of her eyes. What the devil had they been thinking?

He stirred, propped himself up on one elbow and yawned. The covers slipped down around his waist. She longed to crawl in beside him and snuggle for another hour or so. A truly unproductive thought.

"C'mon," she insisted, sweeping up his sweats off the chair and tossing them so they landed against his chest. A very impressive chest it was, too, with that mat of dark brown curls on light bronze muscles. "Put your clothes on." *Please!*

The memory of the feel of him beneath her hands sent a tingle racing through her. That made her antsy. "Get a wiggle on. I'm starving."

She knew the exact nanosecond when the memory

of their near mistake hit him. His whole body tensed. His expression turned wary.

"No way am I going to talk about what happened," she warned. "If you say one word, I swear I'll leave you right here in this room and go have breakfast by myself."

To his credit, Will knew when to exercise caution. He had put on his poker face, and spent the next few minutes sorting out the right end of his sweatshirt by feel and then pulling it over his head.

"Never happened. Agreed?" She left no room for argument.

"Subject closed," he said, his voice brusque. "Have you heard from Eric yet? Did he get Odin's flunky?"

"The guy is a no-show so far. Eric was still out there at the river waiting when he called earlier. Clay was on the way to relieve him so Eric could fly to Atlanta."

"So what now?"

"Breakfast at the restaurant next door. Back here to catch up on the identification process I started at the safe house. I have Eric's laptop and there's a connection at the desk. Shouldn't take long."

"What do you say we order in?" he suggested. "That way you could get right to work, do what you have to do, and we could hit the road."

"Fine." Holly realized then that Will might be self-conscious about feeding himself in public. She guessed that would take some practice if you couldn't see what you were doing. She picked up the phone.

An hour later, well-fed but disgruntled because none of the second crop of photos Mercier sent turned out to be their man, Will and Holly set out for Atlanta.

They made one stop at a small strip mall on the way

and bought sunglasses, a change of clothes and a few toiletries before getting on the interstate.

Will was a little nervous about letting Holly outfit him. "Think conservative," he warned her.

"Red silk boxers with low riders, and a skinny tee. I'll punk your hair for you. You want high tops to go with that?"

"I'll get you for this."

She laughed and rattled a plastic bag with her purchases. "Relax. They aren't Ralph Lauren at these prices, but you'll still be your preppy, low-flash self. I got you some jeans. Everything else is brown. You look good in brown." She stowed the goods in the back seat.

"Thanks," he said grudgingly as she got behind the wheel. "I'll stop complaining, since you're doing all the work."

"Well, use your main talent. Lay out the facts we have and analyze," she suggested.

"My *main* talent, huh? You're sure about that?"

"Oh, hush. You are so typically *male!*"

"I hope so, thank you very much."

She needed to lighten up. Last night had rattled her, too. He knew Holly, and she functioned much more effectively if she could see the humor in something.

Easing all the tension he could and getting them back on an even footing would be the best help he could provide.

"That wasn't exactly a compliment. Don't you guys ever think of anything else besides sex and your appeal to women?"

"Hardly ever," he admitted. "Once in a while, we do divert ourselves with earning a living, but I'm temporarily disabled. At least in that respect."

"Temporarily being the key word," she said. "So how's your vision this morning?"

He turned his head toward the side window as if examining the passing scenery. "You know the French Impressionists?"

"Why are we talking about art?"

"Well, you don't want to talk about sex. *Monet.* Ever seen his paintings?"

She hummed the way he had heard her do so many times when she was searching her memory for something elusive. "Ah, he painted those hazy pastel things. Haystacks, right?"

"And cathedrals, yeah. Fuzzy that up a notch more. That's what I'm currently seeing. Only I'm not sure of the subject matter."

"No outlines yet," she said, not one ounce of pity in her voice, "but better than yesterday, huh?"

"I don't know. Maybe," he admitted. He kept his voice light, unaffected. Inside, he didn't feel light at all. Talking about this was not helping him. Or his attempt to get rid of Holly's extraneous worries so she could focus on the job.

"What are you thinking?" she asked. He sensed she had looked over at him, could imagine her dark eyes widening the way they did whenever she asked a question.

"I'm thinking let's just do this when we stop for the night, and get it out of the way so we don't have to keep dancing around it," he said, shocking himself with the words that had just popped out of his mouth.

He had shocked her, too, obviously. The car jerked minutely to the right before she recovered. "Are you crazy?"

He shrugged and nodded. "I guess so. Think about it."

"Ha!" She switched on the radio and rap blared.

"Oh good, now I'm blind *and* deaf," he grumbled. "Forget it."

"Forgotten," she almost shouted over the so-called music.

He fumbled for the scan button on the radio panel and punched it vigorously until it landed on soft rock. Elevator music. He sat back, folded his arms over his chest and frowned out the window. It was the closest they'd ever come to having a fight.

She waited a few seconds and changed the station again to a jazzy compromise that he tuned out completely. What he had suggested outshouted any sound either of them could summon up.

Think about it. He hadn't quite been able to think about anything else since last night, and knew she wouldn't, either, now that he had brought it out in the open. No inflation of the ego here, just physical facts they couldn't escape. He wanted her.

She wanted him, too. Until they did something about it to ease the tension, neither of them would be worth a plug nickel on the job.

Minutes crawled by. Miles. He estimated a full hour passed without a single word spoken between them as they zoomed down the interstate.

Then she cleared her throat, a nervous sound, one he would never have associated with Holly. "We'll have to stop somewhere first. For…you know."

Protection? She was considering it? He couldn't believe this. He turned toward her, but remained silent.

"One time," she declared firmly. "And don't you read anything more into it than what you said. We get this out of our systems and that's it. That's all.'' He heard her pound a palm on the steering wheel for emphasis.

''Why?'' he asked, before reason could intrude. He wasn't even certain what he was asking about. Why had she agreed? Why was she afraid? Why limit it to a one-night stand?

''Because I said so,'' she snapped. ''Don't push me, Griffin.''

He shook his head. ''Wouldn't dream of it,'' he muttered. But he did dream as they sped along, the vibrations of the wheels on the highway buzzing his body, the sound of a sexy saxophone on the radio insinuating its way into his little mind movie.

One time? Oh no, he didn't think so.

Ground rules had gone right out the window. Holly could hardly keep her mind on the road. The sane part of her brain kept shouting, ''Red alert! Error in progress!'' The impulsive part kept making excuses as it bounced around in anticipation.

She had lost it. Why the devil had she agreed to sleep with Will Griffin?

He was awfully quiet. She risked a glance at him, fully expecting to see a self-satisfied expression on his face.

He was *asleep?* So much for getting him all excited.

She gunned the Jeep and sped around an eighteen wheeler. If she had any sense at all, she would keep driving top speed until they reached Atlanta. Until they met up with Eric Vinland and had a big-mouthed, ever-alert chaperon to keep her from ruining everything.

''Should have kept my trap shut,'' she muttered under her breath. She straightened her arms and clutched the wheel with both hands at twelve o'clock until her knuckles turned white.

"Changed your mind already?" Will asked. He obviously had been playing possum and not sleeping at all.

She huffed. "I thought you might rather *rest* when we get there."

"Yeah, right," he drawled. Then he stretched, laying his left arm along the back of the seats so that his fingers touched her shoulder. He played with the neckline of her shirt, sliding the tip of his pinky under it to tickle her collarbone. "Relax. Where and when is up to you."

He sounded as if he still planned to hold her to it even though he knew she was having second thoughts. She had halfway expected him to back off, maybe even apologize for the suggestion. Will was such a gentleman. But apparently his courtesy was taking the day off.

"You know this is going to be a huge mistake," she said.

"Probably," he agreed. "Scared?"

She rolled her eyes. "Now that's insulting. We're not going to talk about it."

He shrugged. "Fine. There is such a thing as overanalyzing. Kills the spontaneity."

"Right. Better to keep things spontaneous," she agreed for the sake of conversation. She might even talk her way out of this. A part of her wanted to. Another part didn't want him to let her.

"Meanwhile, we've got time to kill. Want to swap war stories?"

"You want to hear about my FBI ops?"

"Not particularly. How about your bust-up with that

guy, the one who made you choose him or the Bureau?"

"No way. That is none of your business."

"Zach Jefferson, I bet. Tell me it wasn't him," Will said, a mocking plea.

"You know Zach?"

"Matt and I went through a training course with him years ago. I know he was with the Bureau. New York, main office, right?" He waited a bit, then added, "And I heard you were with him for a while."

The intelligence community was like a small town, rife with gossip. Now who might he have asked to find that out? And why? she wondered. "So what's so wrong with Zach?"

Will shook his head is disgust. "The tales I could tell you. But I won't. It's all over between you now so it doesn't matter."

"*What* doesn't matter?" she demanded, then immediately scoffed at herself. "You're yanking my chain, aren't you?"

"Caught." He made a face. "Yeah, Jefferson was okay when we knew him. But he must be stupid in at least one respect. He blew it with you."

This flirty side of Will was new. Or maybe she didn't know him quite as well as she'd thought.

"Now you," she ordered. "What dumb floozy broke your little heart?"

"Several, actually. Three to be exact, but I'm not bragging. It's just that I tried more than once. No guts, no glory."

"Uh-oh, where's my violin?"

"I'll admit I didn't really try all that hard. Mostly the job got in the way. You know—phone calls de-

stroying plans, couldn't talk about work. That sort of
thing.''

She figured Zach's problem had been that he knew
the score. As an agent himself, he'd been well aware
that when she went out to work undercover, she faced
real danger, while he worked at his desk and did background investigations. He couldn't deal with that.

Holly wondered what was wrong with those women
of Will's. If any one of them had really loved him,
they should have been able to accept what he did for
a living. He sure seemed worth the trouble to her.

Will hadn't dated any agents or operatives, not seriously or for any length of time, anyway. She had
conducted his background investigation herself before
Jack hired him, and knew that much. ''So it was the
job that sent them running?'' she asked.

He took a full minute to answer. ''I think that the
secretive nature of it made them suspicious. The hours
are so weird and inconsistent. It would be easy to use
that aspect if you were inclined to cheat.''

''You sound a little doubtful. Now you don't believe
that was it?'' Holly guessed.

''Only in part,'' he admitted.

''You were right awhile ago,'' she remarked, her
eyes on the road ahead. ''It's better not to overanalyze
some things. Let's talk about the weather.''

Holly didn't want to know what, other than his work,
had caused Will's relationships to fail. She might have
to admit that the job was only one facet of her failure
with Zach.

Will didn't comment on that little errand Holly had
mentioned, buying protection. He thought he detected
a note of challenge in her voice when she announced

they were at the hotel office and she was going in to register them.

A few minutes later, she got back in the car, said they had a room at the rear, and proceeded to drive around and park. He unfastened his seat belt and got out of the car when she did, waiting for her to lead him to their room.

It was still daylight. They had only driven for about four hours, stopping half an hour ago for gas. This was an unnecessary stop and they both knew it. What they had agreed to do was unwise and they both knew that, too. Will removed his shades. The building was white, the doors painted dark. He could see that much. He thought his vision was a little better, but it was hard to tell.

He hated motel rooms, any rooms where there was only one way out. It seemed sort of symbolic that their little tryst should take place in one. Only one outcome was possible if they went through that particular portal.

"Well, here we are," she said as she closed the door behind him. The heater was on, but it was still chilly in the room. The hum obliterated the sounds of traffic outside.

Holly approached him. The room was too dark for him to see her silhouette, but he could sense her standing just within reach. She wore no perfume, but her scent teased him anyway, causing that low-level arousal he'd been experiencing all day to kick into high gear.

The image of her seemed burned into his brain, the way her lips curved when she smiled, that slow, languid blink she gave when she doubted something he'd said, the hitch of a breath she inhaled when she was about to say something she knew would draw fire. Like now.

"This is…I don't know…awkward." She almost whispered the words. Was nearer than he'd thought.

It was a bad idea, too. Logically, they both knew it. Only his body didn't, and apparently, neither did hers. He reached out and she caught his hand, threading her fingers between his.

He aimed a smile in her direction and shook his head. "You'd go through with this just to keep me from saying you chickened out, wouldn't you?"

She laughed. "Yeah, I guess so. At least that's what I would tell myself. Amberson never backs down, or something to that effect. An excuse."

She kissed him lightly, her breasts barely brushing his chest. "I really want to."

There was nothing to stand in their way, he kept telling himself, yet something kept warning him this would change everything, that it would change him, possibly her, and their world as they knew it.

He pulled her into his arms and kissed her anyway.

He would have this, just this one kiss, full out, no holds barred. Then he'd let her off the hook.

They could surely excuse this kiss as a moment of madness. Maybe they would even laugh it off later, chalk it up to an adrenaline high.

But he hadn't counted on the way her mouth fitted to his, how it coalesced his other senses so they functioned only as accomplices to his one main need.

Her tongue mated with his, matching his eagerness. The sensuous groan she emitted sent hot vibrations singing through his veins.

Her hands slid beneath his shirt, fingers kneading his skin as if they meant to climb inside it. He pulled at her shirt, breaking the kiss only long enough to slip the soft knit over her head.

Their lips met again, a renewed assault. With an expertise not used in a while, he snapped the catch on her bra and raked the straps off her shoulders, sighing into her mouth as skin met skin.

Satin over steel. Her skin, so soft, the muscles beneath so firm and taut. So ready.

He felt her thumbs hook in the waistband of his sweats just as a pounding began. Loud, insistent, unnerving…on the door, not in his head.

"Police! Open up!"

Police? The spell that held Will snapped. Cold air replaced the heat of Holly against his chest. He automatically grabbed for his Glock, but it wasn't there, of course. Hadn't been there for some time now. *Damn!*

"It must be a trick." She pressed firmly on his shoulders. "On the floor! Get down!"

He dropped at once, knowing she'd have enough to do without covering him. Never in his life had Will hated anything more than this helplessness. He couldn't see a freaking thing. Nothing! And Holly had to face the threat alone. Had to protect them both.

"It's okay. You can get up," she said from a distance, probably the far side of the window. "It really *is* the police. Uniforms, patrol car, etcetera."

He stood up and his sweatshirt hit him in the face. He untangled it and quickly pulled it on. He heard the door open.

"Everybody stand back! Hands over your heads. Ma'am, are you all right?" a voice drawled, sounding for all the world like Boss Hogg.

"I'm fine. What's all this about?" Holly asked.

"We had a report that a man forced a woman into

this room.'' Hogg changed his tone and direction. ''You over there, get down on the floor, hands behind you.''

Will assumed the position, unwilling to test Hogg's patience. It would be interesting to see how this played out.

Holly laughed. ''Really, Officer, that's not necessary. He had his hands on my arms when we came in because he can't see. I was leading him inside.''

''Uh-huh. So you're a working girl. Any arrests? Any outstandings?'' Hogg demanded.

''No! I am *not* a prostitute! I'm—''

''Just cool it, girl. We'll see when we run you through the system.''

Will almost felt sorry for the cop. Now he'd made Holly mad. God help the man if he laid a hand on her. Holly was a second degree black belt. She would clean his uniformed clock.

''Get her purse over there and find her ID.''

It was then Will remembered that he had none with him. Holly would have her credentials, though. At the very least, her cover ID.

''She's got two of 'em. Now ain't that interesting? Hey, Raymond, you ever heard of any outfit called Sextant? Sound bogus to you?''

Hogg grunted his agreement. ''Okay, you two gonna have to come on down to the station while we get this figgered out.'' He rattled off the Miranda rights spiel, then asked if they understood.

''I do,'' Holly said, biting out the words. ''And I want you to understand something, you—''

Hogg butted in. ''Impersonating a government official's a federal offense. You cuff him, Ruis. I got *her*.''

Will didn't fight. He kept waiting for the sound of

Holly's resistance, but apparently she was going along with this. He wondered if she was doing that just to avoid finishing what they had started.

Hogg's partner led him out of the motel room and pushed down on his head as he stuffed him in the back seat of the cruiser.

Holly was already there, her sweet scent welcome over the smell of former inhabitants of the vehicle.

Will turned to her. "Got a plan?"

She sighed. "No, but he was waving a .357 Magnum. I didn't want to make his day."

"Smart. What now?"

"He'll call the Bureau, you know. They'll call the office. Everybody will know exactly where we are in a matter of hours, including our insider. Jack's not gonna like this one little bit."

"You don't think it was a regular citizen concerned for your welfare who called this in?"

Holly scoffed. "No. I think someone wanted to see if we're who they think we are. Chief suspect is Odin's friend who was supposed to make sure we never climbed out of the river. He must have seen and followed us from Roanoke."

"No, I don't think he's here. Not yet, anyway," Will argued. "I was probably Odin himself who sicced the cops on us to delay things until his pal could catch up. Last night you paid cash for the hotel? No ID was requested?"

"Right."

"But this time you needed an ID to check us in," he guessed. "And the clerk entered it in the computer?"

"Yes, but it was my cover ID and the company credit card—"

"Which threw up a red flag someplace where Odin has eyes keeping watch," Will finished for her. "And that was a damn quick response time. His mistake, though. Now we know he has access to our list of aliases and—"

"You two stop jawin' back there," Hogg ordered. "You want to talk so blamed bad, save it for when we get down to the station house."

Holly's breath hissed through her teeth. "I want this blowhard buried in the basement of the jail. Naked, with rats."

Will smiled, imagining Hogg at the mercy of rodents. The guy might be better off than at the mercy of Holly Amberson, which was precisely where he would be in an hour or less.

"I wish I could see that," he said under his breath. Holly on a righteous rampage was really something to behold.

They were ushered into the station and cuffed to a couple of wooden chairs to await processing.

"Do we look as disreputable as I feel?" Will asked. They had not taken time to change into the new clothes they'd bought.

"I don't think we've ever looked much worse, except maybe right after we crawled out of the river," she admitted.

For a good hour and a half, they sat there waiting, growing more and more uncomfortable. Then a very polite Officer Ruis addressed Holly. "It's all straightened out. Y'all are free to go. I'll remove your restraints and drive you back to your hotel."

"Thank you," she said, her voice deceptively calm. "First, however, I would like a word with Officer Lloyd."

"Uh, well, uh," Ruis stammered, "he had to leave, see. Another call came—"

"I'll wait," Holly said as the cop removed the restraints from Will's wrists.

Will knew she was loaded for bear. If he didn't step in, this could take awhile, time they really couldn't afford at this point.

He reached out, found her arm and grasped it. "Holly, we need to go."

"Not yet," she said in a clipped voice.

"Yes, *now*. Speed's essential. That call was too convenient. We were set up. He'll be waiting for us." Odin's sweep-up guy had been headed south when he got the call about where they were. That phone call to the local police had ensured that he and Holly would be detained and had provided time to get in place for the kill.

Chapter 8

"You think he'll be waiting for us at the hotel?" Holly asked.

"Probably." Will couldn't guarantee it. He did have a strong feeling there was danger near, but he couldn't get a fix on this guy. Why was that? Maybe it wasn't anything psychic at all in this case, just plain old instinct kicking in, probability knocking.

He heard her take a deep breath and release it with a gust. "Okay, Ruis, let's roll."

"We'll go out the back. This way, please," he said, as deferential as a doorman.

"Get some backup to check it out, Holly," Will insisted.

"He'd be gone before Jack could get anybody here. We need to take this guy alive. It's one on one. I can do that."

"What about your weapon?" he asked.

She laughed, threading her arm through his as they

walked outside. "Wearing them both. They never even frisked me. I was planning to give old Lloyd an embarrassing lesson in apprehension."

"We've got bigger fish to fry, Holly."

She sighed. "Yeah, I know. Got my apron on, honey. Let's set the table."

"Don't try to be cute. You don't need to do this by yourself. I won't let you." The minute the words left his mouth, he knew they were a huge mistake. He had just blown any chance he might have had of talking her out of it. Nobody, but nobody, ever told Holly Amberson she couldn't do anything.

She could, she would and he had no way to stop her.

"You'd do the same thing," she reminded him.

Unfortunately, she was right. They could not afford to lose this opportunity to capture one of Odin's men. Waiting for backup from Jack would take too long. The locals would surround the area and go in with guns blazing if they knew what all this was about. If they didn't, they wouldn't go at all.

Stealth was better. A quiet takedown. Holly was right. Will would have to grit his teeth and pray a lot.

Holly ran every scenario she could think of through her mind as they rode back to the hotel in the patrol car with Officer Ruis.

"If he's there, how do you think he'll play it, Will?"

"He won't be subtle. His orders are to make sure we're dead. He'll open fire the minute we drive up. He might wait until we exit the vehicle, but I doubt it. So what approach are you planning?"

"Back door, of course." She checked her weapon, tucked it inside her waistband again, then pulled the smaller pistol from the holster at her ankle and checked that, too. She'd be facing a fully automatic weapon, the one they had barely dodged at the river, so this could not be a head-on confrontation.

"Ruis, I want you to drop us a couple of blocks away," she said.

"Ma'am, I heard what y'all said. Some dude's gunning for you?" The young officer stared at her, wide-eyed.

She did not need a rookie getting in the way. "Just drop me out of sight of the hotel," she ordered.

"You need more firepower? Hey, I got firepower. Shotgun under the seat," he offered. "Or I can create a distraction, maybe draw him out for you."

"Stay *out* of it," she insisted. "This is not police business."

"This is a good place," Ruis said as he drove around behind a packing company that was closed. He got out of the car and opened the door for her.

Then he pointed off to his left. "See, it's a straight shot from here to the back of the hotel, and you'll have cover from the barrier of trees that flank the interstate. If you want me to, I'll—"

"Thanks, no. Loan me some cuffs."

Ruis handed them to her.

"I want you to stay here, Ruis. Right in this spot, you hear me? I'll have that badge of yours if you don't!"

She turned to Will. "And you, too. If our boy's not there yet, I'll get the Jeep and be back for you in a few minutes."

"We should dump the Jeep," he said.

"Can't. It's Eric's. Besides, if I get this guy, we won't have to worry about that."

"And if you don't?"

"Then we'll call Jack and see what he wants us to do next."

"And if he is there?" Will asked.

"I always get my man."

"Holly…"

"Don't buck me on this, Will. You know I'll stand a better chance if I go in alone."

He held out his hand and she took it. "Trust me, Will. I've got it covered, okay?"

"Right," he said, giving her fingers a squeeze. "Don't be long."

"Back in a few."

No goodbyes. *Assume success. No need for farewells.*

Still, when Will let go of her hand this time, Holly had a galloping desire to run into his arms and promise him she would be careful, that she would be back to finish what they had begun in that room.

Weapon in hand, she slipped soundlessly behind the staggered rows of brushy Virginia pines planted to cut traffic noise. What she wouldn't give to have Will along, his eyes in good working order, providing backup. It must be hell for him, sitting back there in that cruiser with Cop, Jr.

It was not quite dark at five o'clock, but it soon would be. She ignored the prickly needles scraping her face and hands as she worked her way closer to the motel, all the while trying to think like the shooter. Profiling was her strength. Knowing the enemy.

Though she didn't know this guy personally, he wasn't a complete stranger to her. She had listened to his high-pitched voice and heard him decimate the bank over her head with that fully automatic weapon.

He was a hired gun—apparently a loyal one, for a

man like Odin to trust him with completing this job.
That probably meant the two had a history together,
with Odin definitely in a position of command, given
their conversation. Maybe he was an older relative,
military superior or something of that nature.

This man was no leader, and certainly not a planner.
He would employ the most direct, speedy and surefire
method of finishing them off. That meant an unexpected hail of bullets at fairly close range.

If he was waiting for them, she doubted he would
be hiding in the trees or bushes. He'd be a fool to risk
waiting for them in their room. Most likely he would
be in or near his vehicle in the back parking lot, primed
for a quick getaway once he took them out. The on-
ramp to the interstate was only a couple of blocks
away, providing a perfect escape. He could be long
gone before anyone rolled on a 911 call.

Holly parted the branches and peeked out into the
parking lot. There were just half a dozen vehicles and
all appeared vacant. Only one was parked to drive
straight out—a fifteen-year-old Lincoln that she could
probably outrun on foot.

Where the hell *was* he?

Obviously not here, she thought as she continued to
examine the other vehicles just in case he was too stupid to park like a pro, or didn't care whether he was
caught.

There were two cumbersome vans, an ancient
Volkswagen, a shiny new Dodge sedan, the Jeep they
had borrowed from Eric and the old white Lincoln.

She relaxed a little and moved to another vantage
point. Maybe he hadn't arrived yet, could have had car
trouble, or perhaps Odin had problems getting through
to him with the information about where they were.

A distant burst of gunfire riddled the night. The blast of a shotgun. He was at the squad car! *Will!*

Throwing stealth to the winds, Holly ran at top speed back the way she had come, dodging trees, blocking the spiky branches with her free arm. Her mind screamed Will's name while terror closed her throat.

Defenseless. Will had no weapon, no chance. He would be dead before she could reach him.

She raised her weapon, holding it with both hands as she broke free of the tree line and dashed heedlessly into the open when she reached the spot where she had left them.

A burning flare lit the entire area behind the building. Cordite burned her nostrils. Gun smoke hung heavily on the cool night air.

The police car blocked her view of what was going on between it and the other car.

"Will!" she cried, running in a crouch toward the cruiser, using it for cover.

"Down! Holly, stay down!" he shouted.

She fell next to the vehicle and rolled underneath it. Will was crouched on the other side, probably between the car and the door. She could see his feet encased in muddy Nikes.

"I'm here, Will," she gasped, crawling out from under the car to join him, her gaze flying around to assess the situation. The young cop lay huddled next to the back wheel, blood pooling around him.

Will, sheltered behind the open door of the passenger side, appeared unhurt. At least he was still upright.

"You hit?" she asked him, praying.

"No. Are you okay?"

"Fine." Another car, a dark Mercury, sat less than forty feet away, the driver's door open. Halfway between the car and the police cruiser lay the driver, cut nearly in half by the blast of the shotgun Will was still holding.

"It's over, Will," she said. "You got him. Let's see about Junior. He's been hit."

She grabbed Will by the hand and drew him closer to the cop, then unrolled Ruis from his fetal position.

"Put down the shotgun and hold his flashlight." The thing was slippery, covered in blood where Ruis had clutched it to his chest. She directed the beam for Will.

"How bad is it?"

"One, maybe two hits in the shoulder. I'll guide your hand, Will. Apply pressure while I see if he's hit anywhere else."

She found only a nick on his leg, then pressed the officer's collar mike. "We've got an officer down. I repeat, officer down. Request ambulance at 1400 block of Nolan Avenue behind the packing company. Hurry!"

With that, she sat back on her heels and relieved Will of his task. The blood wasn't pumping out, but it hadn't quite stopped. "You're gonna make it, Ruis."

The young man grimaced as he looked up at Will. "Got him, sir?"

"Only because of you," Will said gently. "That was some fancy footwork under fire, Ruis. Not to mention the light display. That flare you shot behind him did the trick."

"Tell…Lloyd, will ya?" Ruis coughed and closed his eyes.

"You bet."

A siren screamed in the distance, growing louder by the second. Holly wanted to throw her arms around Will and hold him tight, rejoice in the fact that by some miracle he was still alive, but there was the kid in uniform, bleeding beneath her hand.

"I knew he'd come for us when the cops released us," Will said angrily. "Why would I think the motel? He had to have trailed us from the station."

"He was a scatterbrained punk, Will. How're you supposed to read half a mind, huh?"

Will crouched there beside her, as he slowly shook his head. "There was no way I could take him alive."

"I don't think either of us could have done that. There's still a chance his identity will lead us to Odin."

Six hours later they were ready to head out again, this time with no plans to stop until they reached Atlanta.

Ruis had made it through surgery. Though his condition was critical, the prognosis was good. Will owed his life to the rookie and felt almost guilty for coming through the incident without so much as a scratch.

The poor kid had emptied his pistol, taking a couple of hits in the process, and still managed to shoot that flare and light things up the way Will ordered. If not for that, they would both be dead now.

Jack had flown in Joe Corda to stay and coordinate with the locals on identifying the shooter, and to control the press.

Jack also insisted that Will have his eyes examined then and there. A brief summary of his medical history arrived by fax, and Will submitted to the necessary scans at the local hospital while Holly hovered with her usual concern.

Now, as she drove down the interstate, she kept urging him to recline his seat and get some sleep.

"They should have given you a sedative," she complained.

"Holly, I'm fine. Not even a headache. Give it a rest, will you?"

"See, you're tense as a piano wire. You never... well, hardly ever...fuss back at me. That just proves my point."

"I'm not fussing at you, Holly," he argued. "In fact, I'm feeling relieved. You heard the doctor. Tissue swelling will continue to go down and my sight should improve." *Should* was the key term here.

The neurologist had qualified her diagnosis with that word, indicating that the results of the tests were hopeful, but not altogether certain. Neither was Will.

His vision had not gotten much better in the last twenty-four hours, or else the improvement was so subtle he couldn't tell it was happening.

He could see blurry silhouettes if the lighting was stark. Proof of that lay in the local morgue back there in that burg. He always hated to get in a kill-or-be-killed situation, but he was glad he had prevailed. This was war and he was trained for that.

Holly was right about the tension. Nothing had ever shaken him up more than having to fire that shotgun at an anonymous target. A raging, moving target, outlined by the glaring light of the flare, spraying death in a wide arc, bent on killing. Will could still feel the man's zeal for it. Not a madness he ever wanted to share mentally again.

He had connected finally, at close range. What did this mean, his linking minds with killers? With a terrorist and traitor?

"Think about something else," Holly ordered, as if

she knew the black thoughts running through his head. "How about some music?" She reached for the radio.

"No, thank you very much," he snapped, remembering that lazy sax stirring him up the last time they had attempted to use music as a distraction. And that memory promptly dished up the torrid scene in the motel room just before the police had showed up to haul them in.

"You know we were lucky we got interrupted," she remarked, attached to his train of thought like a damn caboose.

It was downright spooky. Having your twin do that seemed fairly normal, but the woman you lov…liked?

He scoffed. "Lucky, you say? Pardon me if I don't share your definition of luck."

Holly laughed, but it sounded tentative, uncertain, unlike her usual confident self. "Right now we would have been scrabbling around like crazy, trying to think of something to say to get us back to where we were before."

He heard that thoughtful little hum of hers, then she added, "No, I think it just wasn't meant to be, you know?"

No, he didn't know any such thing. He still wanted her, worse than he ever had before, and he wasn't even aroused at the moment. He wanted to kiss her again, hold her, lie down with her, *be* with her.

Not only did he want her, he needed her. But it wasn't all about him, he realized. What did Holly want and what did she need besides a lover? She had been more than ready to accept him as that, at least on a one-time basis. Unless he was mistaken, she would be again regardless of what she was saying now.

He could please her sexually, he didn't doubt that.

At least he had never had any complaints in that department. It was her other needs that concerned him most.

Who looked after Holly when she wasn't on the job? Her only family was her mother, who had moved back to the Islands. Holly had no social life except for hanging out with him and the other members of the team. She got her nails done weekly and shopped, he supposed. Other than that, her work seemed to be her whole life. She definitely needed more than that.

Why couldn't he be the one? So he didn't have any experience when it came to getting seriously attached to a woman. He could learn. It wouldn't have to be official, if that was what was scaring her.

He couldn't recall ever being able to really talk to a woman about the things he discussed with Holly. They could say just about anything at all to each other. He trusted her. He cared about her.

The couple of feet separating them right now seemed a tremendous chasm he ached to leap, but he didn't quite know how without ruining everything.

Will sensed Holly studying his face, snatching brief glances in his direction to judge his mood, divine his thoughts. She was too damn good at that last effort, he realized, not sure whether it was due to her inherent and uncanny talent at reading people or if she really could ferret out his thoughts by some psychic means.

"I want you," he blurted, figuring he might as well say it outright and be done with it.

Again she laughed, a softer sound this time, a little more self-assured than before. "I know. And you're not used to being denied whatever you want, are you?"

"You make me sound like a spoiled kid," he protested, adjusting his seat belt, running his thumb inside the strap, loosening it over his chest, then crossing his arms over it. "Is that how you see me?"

The Jeep seemed to leap forward, prompting him to brace a hand against the dash. She must be in a hurry to get to Atlanta, to end this conversation. Or land them under a pileup.

When she answered, however, she didn't sound upset, only resigned. "I see you as a man who always gets what he wants one way or another, but you're usually more patient about it, more methodical, too."

"You think I'm manipulative?"

"Determined and persistent," she qualified. "Most of the time I admire the way you stick to your guns until you get results. In this case, though, I think you need to back off for your own good. And mine."

Will ground his teeth, turned his head away from her. "No means no. I got it."

"It can't go anywhere. That's all I'm saying, Will. You know that as well as I do. You said so yourself. Sex for the sake of sex won't work for people like us. For friends and sometime partners."

"I said I got it," he repeated, "so just forget it."

"No, you're not going to think about anything else until we settle it, so let's do that."

"Spare me the reasonable dialogue, all right? You sound like a damn psychologist."

"Only because I am," she reminded him. "And even if my credentials aren't Ivy League like yours, I'm freakin' *good* at it."

"Granted, but I'm not some weirdo perp you need to pigeonhole."

He stifled his anger as best he could, evened his breathing and calmed down a little. Then he looked at her, straining to see more than her dark shape against the car window, trying to visualize her features, her expression.

Would she look sad, contemplative or merely amused?

"So, aside from my obvious and hopefully temporary flaw, what is it about me that puts you off?" he asked, trying to sound offhand.

"I'm not quite that shallow, Will. Your vision or lack of it doesn't enter into the equation and you know it. You also know I'm not put off by you at all. If I were, that sure would simplify everything. At least for me."

"You want me, too. I don't need psychology degrees or a raging ego to determine that." He knew what the problem was and might as well say it. "But you know I'd want more from you than you're willing to give. You don't want to get involved with me. I mean really involved, am I right?"

"Guilty as charged," she admitted. "And you've got the same problem, whether you know it or not."

When he didn't remark on that, she hummed that little hum again, the one that always accompanied her internal meanderings. After a minute, she presented her conclusion. "We have too much going between us already to add intimacy to the mix, Will. It's better if we just let it lie."

She was right, but that didn't make it easier to accept. "Fine. Consider me kissed off," he said evenly.

"Don't be mean, and don't be mad. I admire you more than anybody else I know. I've just decided it's not wise to sleep with you."

Will started to plead his case, then thought better of it. A one-night stand with Holly wouldn't be enough, and what else could they hope to have?

What did he know about successful relationships? He didn't know *any* that were working where the couple had no commitment on paper. Aside from his grandparents, he had never seen any good marriages in operation up close. Jack and Solange Mercier were doing okay for now, as were Joe Corda and his wife, Martine. However, those marriages were new and had not been exposed to the test of time yet.

His parents were a prime example of a match made in hell. Those two had all the advantages a couple could expect, not a single reason for their marriage not to work. Except that whatever they might have once felt for each other had melted away shortly after making twins for the hired help to raise.

Now his mom and dad spent their lives jetting around the world, playing at being ambassadors, spending recklessly and desperately looking for what they had lost. Together, but not really; straying discreetly; carefully avoiding any emotional entanglements. Not with each other and certainly not with their children.

Maybe Will had too little to offer Holly, who definitely deserved a man's full-time, long-term devotion if anybody ever did. He wasn't sure he knew how to give that, even if she would let him. However, deep down he had discovered he wanted to try.

"My parents destroyed one another with their little affair," she said, her voice brisk, her mind running right along the track with his. He was getting used to that, but it was still disconcerting.

"The junior politician and the Jamaican singer," he said, recalling what little he knew of her background. "They did make a beautiful baby."

"Flatterer. I came along after his destruction," she said. "He brought her home with him, determined to make it permanent. Their affair and the mere notion of a mixed marriage wrecked my father's career. I'm sure you know what it was like back then.''

Will nodded. ''It wouldn't be any big thing now.''

''For some people it would,'' she argued. ''It cost him his family and worse. My father took a curve too fast after one of their arguments, and that was that.''

''So you never knew him. What happened then?''

''My mother was stuck in the States, pregnant, and had no money to return home where she might have resumed her job singing at that club where he met her.''

''What about your father's people?''

''You're kidding, right?''

''They are your grandparents. Have you given them a chance to know you?'' he asked gently, remembering how his father's parents had been his greatest comfort growing up.

''Have you made peace with your mom and dad?'' she countered.

He winced. ''Point taken. Then what did your mother do?''

''Took whatever menial jobs she could find. The competition proved too stiff for her to get singing gigs, and that's all she knew. We lived on her minimum wage earnings until I was old enough to help out.''

''I'm sorry it was so hard for you both,'' Will said sincerely, thinking about the young Holly braving that kind of life with only her mother. ''I wish I had known you then.''

''Well, we ran in different circles, didn't we? So there we have it. You and I are not a good idea as a couple, even temporarily. We are way too different. My parents learned that the hard way and learned it too late.''

"You're citing color as an issue for us, Holly? Unless my tan's faded to hospital pallor, I'm darker skinned than you are.''

"Get real, Will. The intensity of the hue is the least of it.'' Her laugh sounded sad.

"Prejudice exists and I'm as aware of that as you are, but you know it's not one of my faults. Race would never be a problem for us.''

"Tell me you never thought about it,'' she challenged, sounding amused.

He smiled. "I've never considered it at all. Not once.''

She didn't respond. Will didn't expand on it, either. What he'd said was perfectly true and she knew it.

Interesting that she related this present situation to that of her parents. Was she considering what might happen to him and herself if they pursued something more than their original plan to heat the sheets for a night? Sure sounded as if it had crossed her mind.

Was he considering it?

Yeah, he was. The idea had already wriggled its way into his mind and was holding on with the tenacity of a pit bull. Will couldn't seem to dislodge it no matter how hard he tried.

Chapter 9

Holly spent the next couple of hours worrying about their conversation and the direction it had taken. This was no time for them to be dealing with the topic. There were just too many other plates in the air right now.

She wearily navigated her way through rush hour traffic on the rain-slick freeway as they reached the outskirts of Atlanta. Her next move should be to stop, call Eric and map out their specific destination. She took the next exit and found a gas station.

Will woke with a start as she braked and cut the engine. "Where are we?" he asked, brushing a hand over his face and through his hair.

"North side of Atlanta. Time to fill up and call in. You want something cold to drink?"

"Bourbon over ice," he quipped, unfastening his seat belt. "But soda will have to do."

A quarter hour later, with the Jeep's GPS set for the

address Eric had provided, they were traversing the
loop around the city past the cutoff for Hartsfield In-
ternational Airport.

By mutual, unspoken agreement, neither approached
the topic they had discussed earlier. They both knew
they would be spared any waffling on their decision by
Eric's presence at the safe house he had selected.

It proved to be a thirties-vintage frame house set in
a neighborhood lined with others very much like it.
Holly knew the dwelling was different in some respects. By now it would have a security system in-
stalled to rival that of Fort Knox, and would be
equipped with state-of-the-art communications gear.

"Home sweet home," she said as she pulled into the
blacktop driveway. She proceeded to describe the place
briefly for Will's benefit.

Eric came out to meet them. "Good news," he said
by way of greeting. "Joe got an ID on the hit man.
He's out of D.C."

Holly rounded the Jeep. Eric grinned at her and
stepped aside with a flourish of his hand to indicate she
should be the one to guide Will inside. Trying to disguise her impatience, she placed Will's hand on her
shoulder. "Let's go."

Will's grasp was light, impersonal, as if they were
strangers. "So can we deduce that's probably also
Odin's base of operations?" he guessed.

"Can't be certain of it, but it stands to reason, especially since we know he's got to have contacts within
the intel community," Eric said. "You need to freshen
up?" he added, looking from one to the other. He held
out the bag he had retrieved from the Jeep's back seat.

"I need a quick shower and a long nap," Holly admitted.

"There are three bedrooms," Eric informed them. "Will you, uh, be sharing?"

"No!" they said in unison.

He laughed. "Hey, no need to sound so horrified by the prospect. Just thought I'd ask."

Holly snatched the bag from his outstretched hand and stalked off toward the hallway, assuming that was where the bathroom would be located.

She refused to stick around and let Eric bait her any further. He seemed to know exactly what she and Will were planning to avoid, and found it funny.

It didn't surprise her that he knew about their little conundrum. It was unlikely that he'd had to use any of his mind-reading tricks to figure it out, though it would be just like him to have done that just to get the particulars.

Even after she closed the bathroom door, she could hear him in there taunting Will, who seemed to be ignoring him.

That was the smartest way to deal with Eric, and about the only way. His pesky kid-brother mentality could be as aggravating as a dripping faucet at times.

Holly quickly turned on the shower, stripped off her clothes and stepped into the tub.

The hot water felt heavenly on her skin. Heat seeped into her muscles, dispelling the part of her tension due to exhaustion, racheting up the rest, which was due to prolonged frustration.

All they needed was a chaperon playing matchmaker. Eric could prove relentless with his innuendos and teasing. He possessed no shame whatsoever when it came to stirring up situations just to watch the results.

There was a madman to apprehend and missiles to

locate. Lives depended on that, and distractions could not be tolerated.

Eric's curious fascination with errant libidos would just have to take a number and wait.

Will plundered the small box of objects Eric had given him, trying to find one that stirred something in the way of psychic connection. They were sitting at the kitchen table, waiting for Holly to finish her shower so he could have a turn at cleanup.

"Nothing," he muttered, tossing a shell casing back with its mates. "This is no good."

"You're trying too hard. You have to relax and clear your mind."

"Then *you* do it!" Will snapped, shoving the container away.

"Don't get so testy. I couldn't get anything from them, either. I figure he only touched these in passing, anyway, most likely wearing gloves. No energy in 'em that I can tell. For me it should be something the subject wore, or at least had some attachment to, however brief. The bigger their emotional investment in it, the better it works. You know, like a kid's teddy bear or—"

"Give it a rest," Will pleaded. "The last thing I want is a lesson in parapsychology, okay?"

He had just about had it with Eric. And his unfounded assumptions about what he called Holly and Will's "newly extended partnership."

They were not even partners, as such, to begin with, though they had joined forces on a couple of missions.

The land line rang. Vinland answered. "Yes?"

Will waited, feeling the excitement build. News from the head shed.

There were no questions on Eric's end. Just a thanks and a click that signaled the conversation was over. Will heard Eric clear his throat and push back his chair. "I better call Holly in here. She'll want to hear this."

"I'm here," she said from the direction of the doorway. Will could smell the peach-scented shampoo, hear the breathless quality of her voice that echoed his own apprehension. Something had broken with the case.

Eric wasted no time. "There's been a hit. A private plane down around Macon, two miles from the airport. Three dead. No survivors. Missile trail and explosion were spotted by a farmer early this morning. He called the Bureau instead of the cops. They investigated and notified Homeland Security immediately. It was a SAM, a Stinger."

"Damn," Will muttered. "Any officials on the plane?"

"No. Two local guys and the pilot, who was from here. Jack figures it for a test run."

"The next strike will be out of Hartsfield," Will said. He didn't know how he knew it, but he did. "Find out who in the government is scheduled to fly in or out of Atlanta on Thanksgiving. The plan is probably to pick a target at random, but…I don't know…it could be they're aiming at someone specific this time."

"We're checking the lists," Vinland said. "You picking up vibes now, Will?"

He shook his head. "No. Well, maybe. But it's not the same as before." He rubbed his skull just below the healing scar. "I somehow sense more than one motive behind all this. Sheer terrorism at its worst, but something else is in play here. I feel it, but it's vague."

"Okay, we'll keep that in mind and see what we can

find out. I'm calling Jack back. Anything I need to add?''

Without thinking, Will said, "Find out who called."

"To report it?'' Eric asked. "I told you, a farmer, then someone from the Bureau. You need names?''

"No, I meant before. When Matt and I were detailed to check out that airfield. I want the names of the informant and who was running him.''

"That second individual is on record,'' Holly told him. "I checked his file myself. It was Lieutenant Colonel Lex Arbin, recently retired from active duty at Fort Meade. He was with Intelligence most of his career. They passed him over a couple of times for promotion to full bird. His son was critically injured when the plane hit the Pentagon.''

"Interesting,'' Will remarked. "But you never interviewed him?''

"Nope. Jack did that himself.'' Holly continued, "In Arbin's call to report Odin's plan, he stated that he got the information from a source who was repaying him for taking care of some incident in Afghanistan. This Odin he mentioned is supposed to be the brains behind the weapons theft, the one running the whole show. Arbin insisted his informant has to remain anonymous for his own protection.''

"The hell with that,'' Will argued, his hunch escalating to full-blown theory. "Let me talk to Jack.''

Eric was already making the call. He handed Will the phone.

When he spoke with Mercier, accepting the reprimand for being in Atlanta and possibly jeopardizing his safety, Will stated his argument for staying on the mission. He might be able to make further contact with Odin if he stayed close enough. And so far, he was the only one who had been successful at that, despite Eric's attempts.

That gained Jack's reluctant and conditional approval. Will could stay in Atlanta, but he had to remain at the safe house.

When he cut the connection and laid down the handset, Will drummed his fingertips on the table for a few seconds. "Jack and Clay are flying down tomorrow morning."

"Glad they're not waiting until Thanksgiving," Eric said with a mirthless chuckle. "So you think this guy Arbin is the insider?"

Holly answered, stating the obvious. "That would be my guess. He might have gained access to the weapons at Picatinny. Certainly would have known where they were. Shoulda been child's play to lift that supply of fully automatics the police had confiscated in the D.C. raids if somebody knew where they were stored.

"And get this," she added. "It was *his* suggestion to have Sextant, Military Intelligence, ATF and the Bureau participate in the joint investigation. He's used to giving orders, I guess."

"And the director agreed to this?" Will asked.

"It was the logical thing to do, what he would have done anyway, most likely. No one was really sure Arbin's information was legitimate, but they couldn't afford to ignore it. So the agents were paired off, as you and Matt were, and sent to investigate. He said it was not a big op, just a splinter group planning to cause a lot of havoc if they got away with the weapons."

"Havoc is right," Will agreed with a huff and a shake of his head. "It's something we've feared would happen at one of our airports sooner or later. There are plenty of shoulder-fired heat-seekers out there unaccounted for besides these.''

''Yeah, they're probably a status symbol for every extremist group around the country. Scary as hell. Anyway, out of the two possible locations Arbin named for the transfer to happen, your airfield was the least feasible. You'll note the MI and Bureau guys were elsewhere at the time of the confrontation.''

''Convenient, splitting up the forces. But it makes no sense that Arbin himself would go to all that trouble to steal the missiles and guns, then blow the entire operation by revealing where the weapons were, and arranging for the bust. If he was bent on revenge or playing out a power trip, why not take the whole load and go ahead and use them instead of keeping only three?'' Eric argued. ''What's the point? D'you think you and Matt were set up as the actual targets that night, Will?''

''We took the bullet, but I doubt it's anything personal. At least not on his part.'' He drummed his fingers faster, an effort to control his hand so he wouldn't make a fist and slam it down on the table.

Control was key here, especially when you wanted to stay in the game, though he couldn't resist adding, ''But you can damn well bet it's personal as far as I'm concerned.''

Holly was already at the computer set up in the adjacent dining room. He could hear her tapping the keys. She would be doing a search on Arbin, pulling up his photo to see whether he was the guy in the hospital.

In less than five minutes, she returned. He heard the crinkle of paper as she shuffled printouts. ''He was obviously disguised, if that was him in the hospital, but

I suppose this could be our man. The height and weight look right.''

Even if they were correct, Will assumed from the conversation they had overheard at the river that Arbin no longer had sole possession of the weapons. The plan was to sell them, and one had already been used. That meant the deal was done.

The most critical thing now was to find Turkel and the two unused missiles. Arbin was the only one who might help do that.

Holly rejoined Will at the kitchen table and placed his hand around a cup of coffee. ''I think Arbin might be the guy, Will. You did good.''

He set down the cup and clasped her hand in his. ''Even if he is, we're not exactly out of the woods. If the colonel is the one and we pick him up, we'll only have the supplier. There are two more missiles out there and a plan in the works to use them.''

''Most likely nearby, too,'' she agreed. She squeezed his fingers, then laced hers through them. He could feel the tips of her nails indent the back of his hand slightly, just enough to make his nerves tingle. Her small palm against his felt warm, intimate.

''Jack, Clay and Eric will take it from here,'' she told him. ''You've done more than your part, and my job is to keep you out of mischief until this is over. We'll hang around in case you get more feelings about this that might be of help, but we're staying out of the action now.''

She was so wrong about that, Will thought as he held her hand and sipped his coffee, not bothering to offer her any verbal argument.

Maybe he couldn't see much, but he wasn't so blind he couldn't function at all without help. And his sight was improving. It *was,* he insisted to himself, gritting his teeth.

No, he wasn't out of this. However long it took, Matt's killer was going to die, even if Will went totally blind and had to beat the bastard to death with a white cane.

"You have to be practical about it, Will," Holly said, sounding worried. She must have sensed his fury. "There's really nothing more you can do."

"Right," he agreed, his voice clipped, his hands steady, his mind flying in all directions at once. "Not now, anyway."

Holly slipped a sedative into Will's next cup of coffee when she poured it. He was wound way too tight, not thinking straight. She blamed herself for adding to that. She never should have responded when he kissed her. She never should have agreed to go to bed with him in that motel.

Every time they touched now—on purpose or not—the act became a jolt of warning for both of them. Yet neither worked very hard to avoid it, or rushed to pull away when it happened. Were they just inveterate danger junkies, or what?

Maybe if they had finished what they'd started, he would be better able to handle this new development now. Or it might have made things worse for him, increased his tension instead of releasing it. She was in nearly as bad a twist as he was.

Trying to talk it out hadn't done one bit of good. They needed to settle things between them and put this out of the way, but first things first.

After he fell asleep on the sofa, she joined Eric in the den just off the kitchen, where he had set up shop.

''Will's down for the count. Anything new?'' she asked. ''Any line on that name Turkel?''

''Nope. Nothing. But now that we suspect who Odin might be and how he was getting his inside info, Jack's putting everybody from Immigration to the profs of Middle Eastern studies onto the problem. Not to mention the CIA, the Bureau, NSA and Interpol. If the name Turkel has ever surfaced, you can bet we'll know where and why within a matter of hours.''

''And Arbin?''

''Pretty soon he won't have any secrets left. If he ever so much as kicked a cat, we'll find out about it. We pulled his military file before,'' Eric told her. ''But now Jack's got people interviewing everybody who knew him, professionally and personally.''

''What about the guy Will shot in Virginia, the hit man? Can they link him to Arbin?''

Eric nodded slowly. ''Yeah. Peter Hackers, a warrant officer who worked in supply. Arbin was an advisor in Iraq while Hackers was there. We're still checking on what Hackers has been up to since he got out last year, but I think we can safely assume the two are somehow connected. Arbin *has* to be Odin.''

''If so, he's bound to be wondering what happened to Hackers,'' Holly said. ''He'll be waiting for word from him that Will and I are out of the picture. When he doesn't get it, that'll surely alert him that something's gone wrong.''

''We have Hackers's cellphone,'' Eric said. ''If anyone calls that number, we're set up to run a trace. As soon as we find Arbin, we're bringing him in.'' He ground a fist into his palm, frowning. ''What's his motive for this, Holly?''

''Greed,'' she said, sure she was right. ''We heard

him mention the sale. They had to get the missiles to the buyer by Thanksgiving in order to collect the money.''

''Yeah, but we've just now verified that Arbin's already *got* money. He's not in debt. Owns his house and two cars and a good portfolio. Why turn traitor and deal with terrorists?'' Eric shook his head. ''No, there's got to be more to it than picking up extra cash.''

''If he has any input about selecting the targets, it could be revenge on the airlines or someone on a particular plane, as Will suggested. A power play, maybe,'' she suggested. ''Boredom?''

Eric rolled his eyes. ''Well, if it is Arbin, we're about to give him more excitement than he can handle, believe me.''

''Soon, I hope.''

''Time for a short break. Jack's calling me back in a few. How're you holding up? You look a little ragged around the edges.''

She rubbed her forehead, trying to smooth out any worry lines, knowing she must look a fright. It had been two days now since she had bothered about her appearance.

Eric nodded in the direction of the living room. ''What's up with Will? Has he been conking out like that often?''

Holly wrinkled her nose, wincing at what she'd done and how Will would react if he found out. ''Not unless I slip him a mickey. He needed the rest, but he wasn't about to be left out of the loop long enough to get it. You know how dogged he can be. I'll have to sit on him to keep him from jumping right in the middle of this with both feet.''

"Sit on him?" Eric said, grinning for real. "Now there's an interesting image. Done it yet?"

She shook her fist at him. "No, and you keep that little mind of yours out of the gutter or you'll be the next one to take an unplanned nap."

"He needs you," Eric said, suddenly turning serious. "Don't be such a hard case about it, Holly."

"I'm not. Will and I both decided it wouldn't be such a good idea."

Eric wasn't buying that, she could tell.

"Jack won't care if you two get involved. Not a hell of a lot he could object to, since he hooked up with Solange, now is there? That was a real rule-bender."

"Let *him* hear you say something like that and you'll be looking for a job."

He ignored that. "All I'm saying is Will's lost his twin. He might have lost his sight, too, as well as the ability to function as an operative if he doesn't get that back. Don't let him slide into depression if there's anything you can do for him, okay?"

It was unlike Eric to admit he worried this much about anything, or anyone. His usual breeziness was an act, of course, or he never would have been chosen for the team, but he maintained that blasé attitude with a vengeance.

"I'll do what I can," she promised. That didn't include becoming a substitute for Will's brother, however, and it certainly wouldn't lead to any therapeutic sex. Will would object to that idea as hotly as she did.

Her agreement seemed to pacify Eric. He went back to the computer and continued his search for information. Moments later the phone rang and he was in deep conversation.

Holly poured herself another cup of coffee. She

needed sleep, too, but knew she wouldn't be able to get any until Eric got off the phone and shared what he was busy finding out.

When Will woke, he would need a status report. The least she could do was to keep him fully informed.

Seven miles away, rain was pouring down. The old house reeked of mildewed rugs, furniture and years worth of decayed leaves that had blown in through the missing roof. Miserable place. Miserable night. Miserable company.

Odin wandered down the stairs to the first floor, where things were a bit less-saturated with rot. The less ancient kitchen wing was intact, leakproof, and provided adequate storage for the Stingers.

The place still stank. The whole operation did, but it would be worth the trouble eventually.

Turkel was kicked back in one of the kitchen chairs, chugging a beer. His two minions were making sandwiches. Of ham.

How quickly they ditched their tenets of faith when exposed to western decadence, Odin thought with a smirk. How fake became their so-called jihad. All they wanted was to destroy and cause chaos, like evil little boys stabbing a big dog through a fence with sharp sticks.

Well, they would soon learn that the fence was not locked and the dog could easily devour them all when the time was right. How he would enjoy that.

Unfortunately, they had to live until Thanksgiving in order to do their deed and assume their rightful blame. Then he could get rid of these turkeys. *Turkeys, Turkel.* The aptness of the comparison made him smile.

Turkel smiled back, a gold tooth shining, a secretive glint of planned betrayal in his black-as-sin eyes.

It was no secret that he hated Americans, even the one who provided him with the weapons to strike a blow for his damn holy war. Maybe especially this one.

That was all right, too, Odin thought as he dug a beer out of the cooler for himself and joined the enemy at the table. All would end exactly as planned, and Turkel and his buddies could complain to Allah in person.

Odin felt righteous about the whole thing. Godlike, really. Everyone was playing his part to the letter. It was a propitious plan, at least for him.

Yeah, it would be worth the collateral damage, worth the sacrifices. He was already doing everything necessary to hold those to a minimum.

Chapter 10

Will woke with a pounding headache that felt like a hangover. A groan escaped when he tried to sit up, and he collapsed back on the lumpy little pillow. Where the hell was he? He opened his eyes cautiously.

The safe house in Atlanta, he remembered. The taste in his mouth gave him a definite clue to what had put him out like a light, and it wasn't anything alcoholic. Damn Holly.

He could make out three windows in the room, but they were indistinct rectangles. No sunshine coming through them, he decided. Streetlights. Dawn or dusk, maybe. Or a very gray day. Not many sounds from outside; must be night. Pushing out a sigh, he sat up.

Again he listened. There was no noise in the house. Neither clicking of computer keys, nor voices. No television.

After a few minutes he heard water pipes gurgle. He

oriented himself as best he could. The kitchen was to his right down the hall, bathroom to the left at the end.

Pushing himself to his feet, shuffling slowly, he felt his way to the bedroom door by sliding his hands along the wall. "Holly, that you?" he called.

A door squeaked open and light flooded the corridor from the other direction, the bathroom.

"Will. You're up early."

Her figure, backlit, moved closer. He smelled the peach-scented shampoo combined with the hand lotion she always used. And her unique scent blended with that, the essence that drove him crazy when he wasn't steeled against it.

Sometimes even when he was.

He propped one hand against the wall to steady himself. "You drugged me," he accused.

"Just a little," she admitted. "Sorry, but you were coiled like a rattler ready to strike." She touched his arm just below his shoulder. "Had to do something. Feel better?"

"Hell no, I don't. I've felt better after weekend frat parties."

He had only vague memories of being hungover in his college days. Never as a Marine. He rarely drank more than a couple of beers at a time now, hated wine and seldom touched hard liquor at all except for an occasional social drink. Inebriation did not blend well with intelligence work.

"Dammit, Holly, I still feel drunk and it's your fault."

She came closer and took his arm. "Come on, baby, I'll get you some tomato juice and a couple of Advil. Fix you right up." She urged him toward the kitchen.

Since he didn't have a lot of choice, he went, sat

where she put him and obediently swallowed the pills she dropped in his hand. The juice calmed his stomach.

She had flipped the light switch when they came into the room. He discovered he could actually make out the placement of furniture, though edges and details were blurred.

He could see her lithe figure moving around. What little he could see, augmented by his other senses, told him she was making coffee, grinding the beans, getting out cups.

It was too soon to shout with relief, he thought. He would still be classified as legally blind according to medical criteria, but this improvement relieved him more than anything had so far. With sufficient light, he was sure he could function without being led around.

"Where's Eric?" he asked.

"He left about an hour ago to coordinate with the feds and the locals. Soon as they get a fix on Arbin, they're bringing him in."

She proceeded to give a rundown on what they had found out. As usual, her report was concise and to the point, with no extraneous data, no conclusions.

"Jack and Clay are arriving around ten. It's 6:00 a.m. now," she informed him when she had finished.

Will ran a hand through his hair and over his face. "I guess I need a shower and shave." He pushed away from the table and stood up.

She touched his arm, but he pulled back, still a little angry with her for sedating him. "I don't need a guide."

"Okay, sure," she said, sounding contrite, but he knew she wasn't. Holly had done what she thought was right, just as she always did. Hell, maybe she *was* right.

Will's head might feel like hell, but he could see a little better now after a few hours of deep sleep.

He walked directly from his chair to the hallway, knowing there was nothing in the way to impede his progress. All he had to do was walk straight back the way they had come and go to the end of the hall to that door she had exited. He could manage that. Nothing to it.

When he reached the open door of the bathroom, he sensed her behind him and turned. "I said I can do this."

"Boy, you sure can!" she exclaimed, grabbing him in a bear hug and kissing him soundly on the cheek. "Will, you can see, can't you!"

"Pretty good," he lied. "So take a hike."

Her delighted laughter and the way she squeezed his arms signaled her relief, made him feel rotten for exaggerating his improvement.

He didn't confess, though. He needed to be left alone right now.

How could he stand having her hover while he took a bath, all the while smelling her, feeling her touch, hearing that sexy little growl of hers? Better to stumble through this by himself than to get stirred up again for nothing.

She was determined to forget what had almost happened between them, and he planned to help her do that. If only he could, too.

Her scent tortured him every time she entered the room where he was. That voice, whether soft or strident, wreaked havoc with his best intentions. He kept picturing how her lips curved when she smiled, how expressive and sensual they were even when she didn't, how lush they felt when he kissed her. His fingers curled at the memory of how smooth she was when he slid his palms over her bare skin. Satin. No, he was not about to forget, no matter how hard he tried.

It helped a little that she had made him mad by doctoring his coffee last night. Maybe he should hold on to that feeling and use it like a safety line.

He stepped into the bathroom and firmly closed the door. The anger was rapidly dissipating in spite of his resolve. Holly had his best interests at heart, he knew. How could he resent her for it?

Will pressed his forehead against the cool wood of the door between them and felt like banging it repeatedly until the pain drove her out of his mind. That probably wouldn't work, either. Nothing did, not even issues of national security.

Holly paced in her bedroom, listening for the water in the shower to stop running. She worked to block out thoughts of him standing under the spray, soaping himself, muscles glistening as they had in the tub at the safe house in Virginia.

Eventually the shower cut off. She shook her head to clear away his image. Water ran again and she heard the tap of a plastic razor against the sink. Could he actually see himself in the mirror now?

Her elation when he had told her he could see much better had faded somewhat. He hadn't managed all that well on his trip to the kitchen earlier.

That frowning, unfocused look he'd been wearing since he woke up from the coma hadn't disappeared. More likely he only wanted her to quit hovering. She could understand that. He must be sick of being dependent on her by now.

She jumped when the door to the bathroom opened,

and quietly moved to stand in the doorway of her bedroom as he emerged. He wore only his sweatpants, the drawstring loose so that the waistband rode low. He kept one hand on the door and reached out to feel for the wall.

His feet were bare. There was something strangely vulnerable about them. They were slightly tanned like the rest of him, though he had paled somewhat during his hospital stay.

He had an almost daily dose of sun in his pool at home, since he swam in all seasons as part of his daily workout. Will was in remarkable shape considering what he had been through. Thank God he was or he'd never have been able to pull her out of that car and the river. She'd be dead now.

"How's the head?" she asked.

He halted immediately, taking his hand off the wall as if embarrassed that she had caught him feeling his way around. "Fine. Still a little foggy from the sedative."

Ah, to explain away his groping, she supposed. "Come and lie down. The bed's this way."

He appeared to be looking straight at her. Maybe she was wrong to think he had lied. Even as she thought that, he walked toward her, his gait natural, confident. He placed his hand on the door frame beside her. "In here?"

She moved back into the room. "Straight ahead," she told him, though his things were in the room behind him.

He made a beeline for the bed, stopped when he reached it, turned and sat down. His gaze wandered around the room. She watched him draw in a deep breath, stretch out his arms and lean back on them.

"This is your room," he remarked, his voice free of any inflection.

"Yes," she admitted, smiling down at him. So he had noticed only her things were in here. He *could* see. Or maybe he realized he had turned left instead of right. Or maybe her scent was stronger in here. "It's mine, but you may as well lie down. Save yourself a trip across the hall."

He stared out the window. "Don't you want to come back to bed?"

"You wish," she said with a teasing laugh. "I'll tuck you in, though, before I go for coffee." She had made a fresh pot when she woke up at five and couldn't go back to sleep. "I'm ready for another cup."

He didn't move when she approached him. He didn't look up at her. But as soon as she was near enough to touch, he grasped her arm and drew her to him, parting his knees so that hers came flush against the bed between them.

He lifted his face to hers, eyes closed. "One kiss," he said, hardly louder than a whisper. "Just to prove we're over our idiocy."

"Are we?" Slowly, inexorably, she leaned down to meet his lips with hers. His were closed, exerting only a gentle pressure when they touched. A sweet kiss, kind and forgiving. Then only giving, a slight increase, an angling of the head, a parting of lips and touch of the tongue.

Holly knew she could pull away if it got too intense. Will was an extremely good kisser, she decided. Probably had lots of practice at gauging his partners' reactions, without getting involved himself.

She enjoyed it for what it was, meeting him on equal

ground, maintaining distance in the small intimacy
while basking in the tactile sensation. That's all it was.

Then his hand slid up her arm, his thumb straying
to the side of her breast, distracting her from the simple
pleasure of his lips. Not simple any longer, she realized
suddenly, her breath catching in her throat.

His mouth had turned hot, wet, just short of demanding. She answered with a foray of her own, unable
to deny herself a little more of him.

He was right here. They were alone. Just a kiss. And
touch, she realized, as his hand closed over her breast
and squeezed. And the other one followed. Under her
shirt.

The sensation of his palms on her bare skin, on her
nipples, sent a shot of lust straight through her. She
pressed into his hands, asking for more.

She meant to pull away. In a minute. But he
stretched back, taking her with him, on top of him.
Then he turned so they lay on their sides, one large
palm on her spine, urging her closer, then onto her
back. He ground his body to hers and she welcomed
it, opened her legs, lifted herself to feel more.

The kiss went on, unending, escalating, encompass-
ing her. Reason became skewed. She didn't care.

This could happen. There was no reason it couldn't.
One time, that was all. Just one time.

They had agreed on that once, hadn't they? She had
agreed. She *did* agree.

With one hand, she blindly grabbed for the small
bag on the nightstand that held the condoms she'd
bought at the gas station. Now he would think she
planned this, bringing him into her room instead of his.

Thoughts melted into need, a frenzied, not-to-be-
denied hunger neither fought. Instead, they battled

clothing, covers, anything that dared impede such a shared craving.

His mouth, that wonderful mouth, strung scorching kisses down her throat, over her chest, closed around her and drew her in. She was inside him.

And with a slow, definitive thrust, he was inside her, too. Holly cried out his name, overwhelmed by sheer gratification. And a feeling of absolute belonging and trust, of mutual giving and getting that defied description.

Sensation billowed through her, building with each stroke of his body, with every clutch of her own around him. Faster and faster he moved until she came apart in his arms, flying free into an unknown zone of pleasure she had never reached before. He gave a final thrust, with a cry of total surrender.

She had never felt so victorious or so conquered, and as if his mind touched hers, in that few seconds she knew he felt exactly the same.

Breathing ceased, muscles collapsed. Little aftershocks of the enormous quake they had survived provided the only movement between them.

"Breathe," he gasped, shifting to one side, their skin slick with perspiration.

"Practical…suggestion," she said when she could form words. Her head was still spinning. Never in her life…

"I'm not sorry," he whispered next to her ear.

Good grief, neither was *she*, Holly thought, but she didn't answer. What could she say?

"Hello?" A shout came from the front of the house.

Oh God. "It's Jack. And Clay," she whispered. "They're early."

This was all she and Will needed, being found in the

sack together. She rolled away from him and snatched up her scattered clothing.

"Just a minute!" she called.

"Everything okay? What's going on?" Jack shouted.

"Nothing! Nothing at all," she answered loudly, putting a cheery note in her voice.

Will raised himself on one elbow, his head in his hand, his narrowed gaze resting somewhere in the vicinity of her breasts.

"Nothing at all? Thanks a lot," he said, his voice tinged with sarcasm.

She was dancing around awkwardly, trying to get her feet in the legs of her slacks. "Don't mention it," she snapped as she jerked up her pants and zipped them.

She yanked her shirt on over her head and plowed her fingers through her hair. "I mean, seriously, don't ever, *ever* mention it."

He grabbed the quilt, pulled it up to cover himself, and rolled over so she couldn't see his face. Great, now she had insulted him. Men were way too sensitive when it came to performance. How could he not *know* how great he was in bed?

Well, she would have to reassure him later, because right now she had to cover for them if she could.

Holly stuck her feet in her shoes and marched out of the bedroom, her skin still tingling from the delicious climax.

Damn Will, anyway. What did he expect her to do—wait in there, propped up against the headboard next to him to greet their boss?

Jack wasted no time in delivering the data he had acquired on Arbin and Hackers, but he kept giving her that look. She knew he knew.

Holly pretended to focus all her attention on the photos and faxed reports he had spread out on the kitchen table. Clay remained silent, almost grim. He knew, too.

Or maybe she was just paranoid. How could they know? The scent of sex on her, maybe, but the smell of the burned coffee was pretty strong.

She ran a hand over her neck. No beard burn. Will had just shaved. Her hair was too short and curly to be all that mussed, and she wasn't wearing any makeup to be smeared.

With a tremendous effort, she shoved the worry aside and concentrated on what Jack was saying.

"Turkel's name came up, but it's most likely an alias. He's probably a sleeper, but we don't know for whom. We do know he's lived in the States for at least fifteen years, and we have one photo, group shot and not very clear, taken at a mosque in Atlanta right after the New York attack. That's about all we've got."

He picked the photo out of the stack and placed it in front of her. "I take it that's not the guy in the hospital?"

"No, he was definitely Caucasian," she replied. "I think it was probably Arbin I saw, though he was disguised if it was."

"Eric told me. You think you could give a positive ID if you saw him in person?"

"Probably. Have they found him yet?"

"Not yet. He could be anywhere in the world by now. Every agency is all over this with all available personnel looking for both Arbin and Turkel."

"It'll be a miracle if they find Turkel. He could be set up anywhere," she said.

"It's likely he's within a five-mile radius of the airport. Any farther out and using the Stinger successfully might prove problematic, since it's one of the older models. Right after takeoffs and just before landings are the optimum strike zones. Planes are moving slower and it's easier to identify them then."

He collected and stacked the photos and paperwork, laying them to one side in a neat pile. Then he crossed his arms on the table and leaned forward, his eyes narrowed. "Now then. How's your mission progressing?"

She almost gulped, but managed to don her best poker face. "Will's vision is better, he says. And he...he seems to be getting his strength back."

Clay gave a grunt that sounded almost like a chuckle. If Will was usually quiet and reserved, Clay was even more so. His strongly chiseled Native American features betrayed no emotion whatsoever unless he was working at it.

He played to his heritage, wanting everyone to see him as the invincible, stoic warrior. She usually loved trying to shake him up, surprise him, make him laugh. Right now she was not in the mood. She shot him a nasty look.

Jack persisted. "Is he getting enough rest?"

"Absolutely. Will's in bed right now." Oops. Wrong thing to say.

Jack gave her that tongue-in-cheek look again as he continued to stare at her, making her nervous as a cat. "Clay, would you excuse us, please?" he said without glancing away from Holly.

Clay rose without a word and headed down the hallway, his steps silent. Holly heard the click of a door closing.

Jack cleared his throat. "Stop looking as though I'm about to rip your head off, Holly. I'm only worried about how this could affect you and Will. And the team, of course. It's very easy to get caught up in something when excitement's running high, and then later regret it.''

She shrugged. "Well, you did order me to look after him. I've been doing that.'' Deliberately, she neglected to mention that he himself had been caught up in something on his last big mission. Something that had resulted in marriage. Did he regret it?

Jack was shaking his head. "Solange and I have worked it out. So have Joe and Martine. Will would worry about you the way we would worry about them if they were in dangerous occupations. It could compromise his effectiveness in the field.''

"That's sexist tripe and you know it, Jack, and I'm surprised at you. You think your wives don't worry about you when you and Joe go out? How does that impact on their jobs? Ever thought about that?''

"They know we can handle ourselves.''

"And Will knows I can, too. I've probably had more field missions and experience in firefights than either you or Will have. He trusts my abilities.''

"Yes, but that could change if he falls for you, Holly.''

She gave up; there was no point arguing with him when it was all over, anyway. "I know. This was a temporary thing.''

"Was?" he repeated.

"Was. As in a one-time occurrence. So set your mind at rest. He and I are back to buddy status, and that's it. No need to ream him out about it, or even to bring it up. This was my bad, okay? It's over.''

After a few moments assessment, Jack nodded. "Duly noted.''

* * *

With only one clue, Will knew who had entered the room. A very faint smoky scent of sage surrounded Clay unless he was actually going into the field. Then he was undetectable in all respects unless he wanted to be noticed.

Now he was waiting for Will to acknowledge him. "Clay," Will said.

"You can hurt her."

"I would never do that," he answered.

"Intent does not predict outcome."

"Spare me your old grandfather's nebulous sayings," Will grumbled. "They sound strangely like Confucius, and I think that's the wrong tribe."

"It is a truth, regardless of the source."

Will sat up, crossing his arms over his chest. "Hit Holly with it and see what she says."

Clay grunted. "She would tell me my pigtails are too tight."

Will couldn't stifle a laugh. "Yeah, I expect she would. What do you see ahead for us that's so bad, Clay?"

"Nothing. But you know how it goes. Alone is better in what we do." The resignation in his voice was in no way concealed. Nor was the sadness.

What had happened to him? Will had no information about Clay's background other than what Jack had revealed along with his qualifications when he was hired. Raised on a reservation, special scholarship, uncanny ability with languages, tracking of all kinds including electronic, and hell on any kind of wheels.

"This was only a brief break in the aloneness," Will assured him. "We're allowed that once in a while, don't you think?"

A long silence ensued, then Will sensed movement. He could see Clay's tall form limned in sunlight, and tried to make out his face. It was impossible.

He kept attempting to focus while Clay left the room as silently as he had entered.

Will figured he might as well face the music with Jack and get it over with. He rolled off the bed, felt around for his sweats, found and pulled them on. It wouldn't hurt to be fully dressed for this, he thought.

His room was the one across the hall. Will could see the shape of the door and made for it, striding instead of groping tentatively as he had been doing. Near as he could tell, there was nothing in his way.

Despite the exhausting lovemaking with Holly, he felt energized. Her hasty exit and apparent shame at what they had done still ticked him off, but he would survive that.

What had he expected—for her to fall madly in love with him after one roll in the hay? Holly didn't do love. And neither did he.

The doors to the rooms were offset, not directly across the corridor, and he almost walked into the wall, but put his hand out just in time.

In a matter of minutes, he had found the sports bag they'd bought for his change of clothes, and put on the new jeans and shirt.

He felt marginally better able to greet the world. Now if he could just get to the other end of the house without breaking his neck...

Will trailed one hand along the wall until he reached the well-lit living room and could see the kitchen door. He approached it, arms at his sides.

He didn't expect to fool anybody for long, but it just

felt more normal not having to grope in front of him with a vacant look on his face. He could discern where people's heads were if the light was good. Might as well pretend he was looking them in the eye.

He thought there were two people sitting at the table, but couldn't be sure. There wasn't enough contrast. "So, what's up?" he asked, sounding a little belligerent, more so than he meant to.

"Holly will fill you in later," Jack said. "Right now I need your help."

Well, that was a surprise. "With what?" He squinted at the jumbled shapes again and went for what he took to be a chair back. Luckily, it was. He dragged the chair out and sat down, keeping his eyes lowered.

"We have some clothing appropriated from Arbin's apartment in D.C. I want you to try to make a connection. Eric's not here," Jack told him.

"I haven't had any success with that," Will warned him.

"Neither did he with the shell casings. But those aren't personal items. There were no prints on them, anyway, so Arbin probably only touched them with gloves. Try this."

He placed what felt like an article of clothing in Will's hands.

No amount of clutching or fondling produced anything. He lifted it to his face and sniffed. "Old-fashioned Bay Rum, I think." Not even a trace of body odor. "No starch. Cling fabric softener."

"Thank you, Martha Stewart," Holly quipped.

"You're welcome. So lock me up, but I've got no insider info from this, okay?" He tossed the garment aside. "Sorry."

"It's all right," Jack said, his impatience evident. "Maybe we're barking up the wrong tree, anyway. We'll get Eric to try when he gets here. Have you had any further psychic experiences since you felt Odin approach the safe house?"

Will thought about it, but then Holly answered for him. "He was sure the shooter would catch up to us, and said so when we were still at the police station."

She sounded so proud of him. Didn't she understand how iffy this psychic thing was? How unreliable and easy to misinterpret?

Will tried to explain that. "But I had no clue that he would follow us from the station. I had it in my mind he would be waiting at the hotel, and that nearly got us killed. How's the cop, Ruis?"

"Downgraded from critical to serious. He'll make it. Did you actually see the perp you shot?"

"Silhouette only. And the gunfire. I aimed for the body," Will admitted.

"Can you see much now?" Jack asked.

Will hesitated over the painful admission. "Not really."

"So stop pretending," Holly ordered. "You got me all excited for nothing."

He kept his mouth shut, not about to touch that line.

Jack was watching him; Will could feel it. Now he would get the lecture, but he suddenly didn't care. What did it matter? He'd be out on his butt soon anyway, off the team, sitting around somewhere learning braille, waiting for experts to train his new guide dog.

Time to stop kidding himself. This latest improvement could be as good as it got.

The flash of self-pity disgusted him. He couldn't give in to that. If he gave up and admitted he was blind, that would make it so. "It's gradually coming back. Just not as quickly as I had hoped."

"At least it's happening," Jack said, sounding relieved. "Clay can drive you to the airport first thing in the morning. You and Holly are flying to Walter Reed so you can have further tests."

"No!" Will exclaimed. He realized Holly's own protest had coincided with his.

"Why not?" Jack asked reasonably.

"Because I might be needed here. I'll go right after we get Turkel and the missiles," Will insisted.

"Besides, if we don't get them," Holly added, "won't all commercial flights be canceled?"

"Not until just before midnight tomorrow. The next day is Thanksgiving," Jack said. "Announcing that we're doing that will cause mass pandemonium, not to mention what it will do to the economy in the days to come."

"I need to stay, Jack," Will declared. He had a feeling, a compelling urge he had to follow. "Something's telling me to stay."

Chapter 11

Jack gave in. Holly couldn't decide whether she was relieved or not, but she felt she owed it to Will to side with him in this. They had come this far.

He had taken up Arbin's shirt again, a grim look on his face as he clutched the wrinkled fabric in his hands. She could feel his desperation to make some kind of contact.

Suddenly he stood up, still holding it in one hand. "Let's take a ride."

"You got something?" she asked.

"No. Just a vague feeling that I need to get outside for a while. To *do* something," he added. "It can't hurt to run with it, right?"

Holly grabbed her purse and the keys to Eric's Jeep. "Let's go."

She stopped long enough to shoot a questioning look at Jack, to see if he had any instructions or ideas.

He frowned, obviously doubtful that this would lead

anywhere. Though she knew he was a staunch believer in psychic abilities, he probably thought Will was now grasping at straws. "Clay and I will be here when you get back, unless something breaks in the meantime. We have reservations at the Marriot downtown for tonight, but we can hang around for a few hours. Call if you need us."

In the car, Will seemed preoccupied, maybe a little despondent. He gave her no directions, so she headed for the loop that encircled the city, hoping against hope that something would occur to him as they rode around it.

"Tonight's the night," Will muttered.

"What?"

"Tonight," Will repeated. "Something will happen. He's excited."

Will put the shirt in his lap and reached up to rub his temples. "Where *is* he?"

Holly remained quiet, navigating through the traffic with practiced ease. She made no comment when Will laid his palms flat on his thighs, where the shirt lay crumpled.

He leaned back against the headrest, eyes closed.

"Columns," Will growled, as if furious. "A house with columns. He's watching it. Can hardly wait to kill."

"What else does he see?" Holly asked, her voice soft, as unintrusive as she could make it. Will seemed in some kind of hypnotic state, so she tried to work it. "He sees the house and…"

"Trees. A van. He's inside the van. Gun on the seat. An AK-47. His hand is on it."

Suddenly, Will straightened and shook his head as if the spell had broken. Holly almost cursed out loud.

"Back to the safe house," he ordered, his tone urgent.

She didn't question it. At the next exit, she veered to the right, crossed under the highway and reversed their direction.

Her cellphone buzzed and she activated the speaker. "Amberson."

"Arbin just called the local Bureau and they routed him to us," Jack said. "He thinks he's located Odin."

After Holly hung up, she knew she had better question Will while his vision was fresh and before parts of it faded the way dreams did.

"Go over it now, Will. I need you to tell me everything you saw."

"Everything *he* saw. It's as if I'm looking at things through his eyes." He shook his head again. "Damn! It gives me a headache." But he dutifully detailed everything, including the swells of emotion that had gone along with it.

Nothing new emerged, but toward the end, there was serious frustration in his tone. "His voice at the river— I keep thinking about it." Will pounded a fist on his thigh. "It sounded so…familiar. I can't place it, but that voice…"

"Maybe if I describe him to you again it would spark something." She recounted the features in the photo, and also how the man had looked in the hospital, with the wig, mustache and heavy jowls.

She was pretty sure they were the same guy. Similar height of about five-ten, sloped shoulders and wiry eyebrows.

Going over it all now, she realized that in both guises, he was a fairly average looking guy.

"Doesn't help," Will said after thinking for a minute. "Could be just about anyone."

"Try not to dwell on it so much, and recognition might come to you if he is someone you know," she advised. "Think about something else that's totally unrelated."

"Not too difficult," he muttered with a dark scowl.

"Don't think about *that,* either," she warned.

He grunted, a half chuckle. "You're the mind reader now? How do you know what I was talking about?"

She clicked her tongue and shifted uncomfortably. "Because even with everything else going on around us, it's all I can do to keep my own mind off of it. We agreed only once, and then we'd forget it happened, right?"

"Easier said than done, but I'm working on it," he answered.

Holly couldn't let it go like this. If they let that single episode of intimacy affect their work in a negative way, Jack would drop one or both of them from the team. He would never tolerate less than their undivided efforts no matter what, especially right now.

"Look, Will, don't be mad. I'm not saying you weren't great in bed. Spectacular, in fact, but—"

"Spare me the buts. My ego's not the problem."

"Then what *is,* for heaven's sake? What are you so angry about?"

He released a gusty sigh. "I don't know. That's no lie, either. I really don't."

She believed him. He looked about as confused as she felt.

He had been through hell these past few days. Finding out about Matt's death, his faulty vision, the mad scramble and slam dunk in the river. The shootout when he could barely see the target… And now dealing with this newfound mind link with a killer.

Add unwise and unexpected sex to that cocktail and it was small wonder he was ready to snap at her, or anyone else who was handy.

She reached over and gently squeezed his arm. "Well, just try to keep a lid on it, whatever it is. At least until this is over. Then we'll have this out and settle it once and for all, okay?"

He covered her hand with his. "I'm not angry with you," he said, his voice gravelly and quiet. "And I'm still not sorry it happened."

She smiled to herself, trying not to, but his words were reassuring, settling comfortably around her heart like a warm blanket. The smile faded as quickly as it had formed. Those words and that tone of his also migrated to other regions and made her deliciously uncomfortable.

Jack, Clay and Eric were waiting for them when they arrived at the safe house. She led Will by the hand as they entered. "What's happened?"

"Arbin called again," Jack announced. "Georgia Bureau of Investigation agents found the site where he first said he thought Turkel was located, but it's been abandoned. They did get some good prints to work with in identifying Turkel and the others, if they're in the databases, but that's probably going to be too little too late."

"So it's confirmed that Arbin's on our side? He's been working this from the beginning?" Holly asked.

"Apparently he took it upon himself to go under-cover when the opportunity presented itself. That's what he's claiming. He's not trying to avoid questioning, he says, but he can't come in yet and won't reveal where he is."

"No trace possible on his phone?" Will asked.

"It's a cellular, but not top of the line. If we can get him to call here directly and he's not moving around, we can trace it."

"He wants full credit for the capture," Holly surmised.

"Maybe," Jack said. "But he would get credit, even with full backup from everybody on the op. Something's hinky about this whole thing."

Holly explained Will's vision in the car as quickly and concisely as possible, then added, "So we need to concentrate on the outlying areas. Get a fix on any isolated houses with columns."

Eric laughed. "Holly, you do know where we are, don't you? Are there any houses measuring over a thousand square feet in this county *without* columns?"

It seemed hopeless. Holly gave up for the moment and went to make a fresh pot of coffee. In situations like this, a shot of caffeine sometimes helped stimulate ideas.

"Where are you dragging me now?" Will asked.

She realized she was still holding his hand. With everyone on the team standing there watching. And after Will had proved earlier that he could get around inside the house perfectly well without being led.

She disentangled their fingers and tried to laugh it off. "Sorry. Force of habit."

The day crawled by. Will felt he should be doing something, but he also knew there was little that even the other members of Sextant could do at the moment. Holly had ordered him to rest. He lay propped against the headboard of his bed on several pillows, but found he was unable to turn off the worries and sleep.

The team's main job lay in prevention of terrorist activities, and usually involved infiltration into the organization. They'd gotten in on this too late. Will figured he was the one doing the closest thing to infiltrating with this mind reading of his. It was not enough.

Agents from all the major organizations were running down leads, combing the area around the airport. SWAT teams were alerted and standing by. Snipers, too.

Things could break at any minute. Or maybe they would break too late, with a planeful of passengers already down. That could happen tonight or tomorrow if the attack was planned for Thanksgiving.

He rubbed the back of his neck, feeling the tension, the ache caused by concentrating too hard too long. A cold drink was what he needed.

Barefoot, taking it slowly, Will headed for the kitchen. As he walked down the hall, he could hear Clay talking—unusually verbal for him, though he was speaking too quietly to be understood.

Will had just reached the end of the hallway when he heard his name mentioned.

"Will's in no condition to be making decisions," Clay was saying.

So they were planning to keep him out of things altogether. He stopped where he was, leaned back against the wall and listened, gaining some time to formulate his arguments before going in.

"What happened was not exactly a carefully considered decision," Holly announced. "And even if we had thought it out and made a wrong one, this is between Will and me. Our business, you got that?''

They weren't talking about the job, Will realized.

Clay persevered as only Clay could. ''You need to think about what would be involved here. There are not only potential complications at work, but imagine all the cultural differences you would have to resolve. Even you and I have more in common than the two of you do.''

Holly laughed at that. ''You from the res, me from the projects? I don't think that's solid ground for compatibility, Clay. Will might have been born gumming a silver spoon, but he and I manage to get along okay.''

''Now, maybe,'' he said, a warning in his tone for what the future could bring.

''You're assuming way too much about how far this has gone.''

''I would never say anything if I didn't care about you, Holly,'' Clay said quietly.

Will grimaced. So that's how it was. That's why Clay had advised him to remain a loner, huh? So much for friendship and loyalty. Screw Clay Senate.

A swift wave of jealousy engulfed Will, almost prompting him to stalk into the kitchen and punch Clay out. But he didn't.

In the first place, he'd probably swing and miss. In the second, Holly would take him down before he made contact, and embarrass the hell out of him. In the third, Clay was right that Holly should think twice.

To hell with the social differences he had mentioned—that was nothing. But Holly did deserve someone who was all there and functioning fully.

Will knew his days with Sextant were numbered if he didn't recover completely. If he were forced into medical retirement, the only logical place for him to go was back to upstate New York. He owned a cabin and some property on Shroon Lake, near the family estate.

Quietly, he backtracked to the bedroom, not wanting to stay and hear Holly's response, or more of Clay's avowals. And that surprising jolt of jealousy didn't diminish one little bit.

It was then Will realized that Holly meant more to him than he had thought. More than like. More than admiration. More than lust. He refused to give what he felt a name. Banishing it would be easier if he didn't admit it.

She joined him before he reached the bed. "Will? Was that you in the hall? Did you need something?"

Did he *need* anything? Yeah, but he wouldn't take it even if she offered. He shook his head, not trusting himself to speak.

He sat down on the edge of the bed, turning his face to her as if he could see clearly. Blurred as it was, he could still visualize her worry.

"You overheard us," she guessed. "Clay's concerned, that's all."

No, that was *not* all, by a long shot. But Will didn't want to argue, not in his present state of mind. What could he say? *Yes, Holly, you and I would be a match made in heaven?* Not hardly.

"It's okay," he said instead, forcing a smile. "He gave me the lecture, too."

She plopped down on the bed next to him, her leg resting solidly against his. He had the urge to pull her down and stake a claim, as stupid as that would be.

"Clay's talked more today than in all the time I've

known him,'' she said with a little laugh. ''Surprising to find out he's such a big buttinsky.''

''That's not all he is. He's hot for you himself.''

Her snort was inelegant. ''What? You're crazy! Clay's a good friend, Will, and he's worried, that's all. He's warning us off each other as if he thinks we're hooking up permanently or something. I told him it was just temporary insanity and *over*.'' She stressed the last word, drawing it out.

''You'd have the same issues with him,'' Will announced in spite of himself. He sounded surly, like a kid denied a treat and having to watch it given to someone else. He shook his head and tried to temper his tone a little. ''All I'm saying is that Clay's great, but he's wrong for you.''

She shoved herself off the bed. ''Not you, too! I'm getting really sick of people telling me what's good for me and what's not, y'know? You and Clay and Jack can just go…eat dirt!''

Will smiled briefly. Holly very seldom lost her temper, but when it flared, her invective skills suffered. When she kept her cool and employed her sharp, sarcastic wit, she could skin the hide off an opponent before he knew he'd been flayed.

At least she had lumped Clay in with the doghouse crowd. That was something. However, Will feared that when she stopped to think about it, she might seriously reconsider all their teammate had said.

Even if he did get his vision straightened out maybe he should think about leaving Sextant, Will mused. As much as he loved the job, Holly had seniority, so he should be the one to go. He could return to ATF. If he did, Holly might see him as something more desirable than temporary insanity.

He heard the phone ringing, but tried to ignore it. If he began distancing himself now, both from the job and from Holly, it might eventually be easier to come to terms with losing one or probably both.

The prospect of the effort left an empty place inside him that he knew would take time to fill.

"Will!" Holly cried as she hurried back into the room. "Arbin called again. Jack says we've got a trace! He's over near Decatur."

Will was already on his feet, sliding them into the shoes he had left by the nightstand. "Let's go."

Her palm flattened against his chest. "Wait. Uh, you and I are supposed to stay here and...answer the phones."

Will bit off a curse and moved around her, breaking contact. He was wound so tight he was grinding his teeth. He needed in on this op so bad he could taste it, but what could he do?

"You'll follow orders and provide support," Holly told him, following right behind him as he strode toward the kitchen, where Jack and Clay would be preparing to leave. "Team players, remember?"

Everyone in the new organization had had to take lessons in teamwork. Several dangerous ops had taught them the value of that. They had all been loners of sorts when hired by Sextant. All but Will. He'd had Matt.

Will realized that leaving ATF and taking the job with Sextant had been his bid for independence from his twin. They had reached age thirty and had rarely been apart more than a week at a time. Even Matt had agreed he sometimes felt like a bookend.

They had teamed up again to represent their two agencies at the beginning of this mission, Matt's last. Dammit, Will needed to see this through to the bitter end. And he did not want to do it sitting in this cozy little kitchen waiting for the phone to ring and let him know it was over.

They had hauled in the bin Will knew Jack would have shipped with the weapons and gear. He recognized the familiar rip of opening and fastening Velcro straps. Clay and Jack were donning their Kevlar vests.

The ejection and replacement of clips in the nine millimeters came next. Then the loading of their backups.

Will mentally ran through all the steps of preparation himself, his fingers clenching at the unaccustomed inactivity. God, he needed to *do* something.

Holly slid a hand through the crook of his elbow, her long nails biting gently through his shirtsleeve. A gesture of comfort, pity or restraint? Whatever, he had to stifle the urge to pull away.

Jack spoke then, above the rustle of packs being shouldered. "I sincerely hope this won't turn into the circus I'm afraid it might."

"There'll be a bunch of trigger-happy glory seekers out there, I bet," Holly said.

"More badges than you can shake a stick at," Clay muttered.

"Pancakes for breakfast, so don't dawdle," Holly declared brightly.

She squeezed Will's arm, prompting him to say something, he guessed, but he couldn't. Not when he wanted more than anything to be going out that door himself.

No goodbyes again. It would be business as usual, and they'd hook up again in a little while.

"See you two later," Jack said, his voice fading as he left through the back door.

"Keep the coffee hot," Clay said. "And your feet on the floor," he added meaningfully.

Will would have gone after him if Holly hadn't grabbed his arm with both hands. She was laughing, damn her.

"Freaking clown!" Will growled.

Still chuckling, she pushed him down into a kitchen chair, her hands on his shoulders. "Chill. He's just teasing. If he'd said something like that a month ago, you'd have thought it was hilarious."

"It's not the least bit funny *now*."

He knew she had begun clearing away the unused stuff piled on the table when Clay and Jack were getting ready. Unnecessary clutter always bothered her.

She was something of a neat freak, another thing they didn't have in common. His messiness came from having hired help to pick up after him in his early years, he guessed. Holly had never had that. As far as he knew, no maid had ever entered a place where Holly lived.

He propped his arm on the table and massaged his eyes. He squinted at whatever she had just massed in the middle of the table and tried to make out the objects. A low, squat sugar bowl. Salt and pepper shakers, tall and skinny. He reached out and touched them to be sure.

After staring hard for a few seconds he realized the edges and details were only slightly fuzzy. Everything around them remained out of focus, but he could see the shakers.

He refused to get too excited, but this was the first time anything had appeared this clearly to him since the shooting.

He wondered briefly if maybe he had a psychosomatic problem instead of something physical due to the injury. No, his sight had been improving steadily. This was just another milestone, like when he could differentiate light and dark. And colors. His excitement mounted.

Blinking rapidly, then squinting again, he trained his vision on something on the far side of the room, a dark shape against the wall. He stared hard.

"Pie safe," he muttered in wonder as the porcelain knobs crystallized, white against dark wood.

"Hmm?" Holly asked, sounding distracted by what she was doing.

Will hesitated, then risked jinxing his luck by voicing it. "I...I can see the pie safe over there. The knobs on it."

He turned to her, suddenly desperate to touch her with all his senses. After a few seconds, her wavering image steadied. "Stop frowning," he said, his own smile tentative.

She rushed toward him around the table, ruining his focus and destroying the clarity he had gained. "Oh, Will, it's back? A miracle!"

He caught her waist as her hands landed on his shoulders. "No, nothing miraculous yet," he protested. "I just haven't tried that hard to focus until now, not since yesterday. Too frustrating. But the light's pretty bright in here and if I hone in just right, I get a small field that's fairly clear. Tunnel vision, I guess you'd call it."

He narrowed that on her face as she looked down at him. "You're not smiling yet."

She beamed suddenly, her straight white teeth gleaming, her eyes swimming with tears. Dimples flashed in her smooth, creamy cheeks. "I am so relieved,'' she sighed, cradling his face with her hands. "You'll get it all back soon, Will. I *know* it."

"None too soon for me," he said with a huff. "If this had happened earlier, we could be—"

She sat right down on his lap, shocking him into silence. Her arms looped around his neck. "No, we couldn't. You're not ready for that yet. Hush about the op. We've got our orders. Now you can get that enormous chip off your shoulder.''

The chip was not his main problem at the moment.

She brushed the hair off his forehead with her finger. Her face was close enough that he could distinguish the individual features pretty clearly.

He couldn't help but revel in the fullness of those lush lips, the liquid warmth of her doe-brown eyes beneath the lazy sweep of long black lashes. "You are so beautiful. Did I ever think to tell you that?''

The firm curves of her buttocks pressing against his lap shifted, wriggling for a comfier spot. Comfortable for her, maybe, not for him. Suddenly he was hard as a rock, and no way could she be unaware of that. "Holly?"

"Yeah, Will?" she whispered.

"What are we doing?"

She brushed her lips over his as she answered, "Celebrating. Lettin' off steam."

It must be coming out of his ears by now. "More insanity?''

"Sure, that would be nice," she mumbled, the words all but unintelligible as he took them in his mouth.

Sheer hunger grabbed him with talons that dug deep, refused to let go. He wanted to sweep her up in his arms and haul her into the bedroom. Or take her right where they sat.

Her breasts nestled into his palms as he cupped them through her soft T-shirt. She wore a sports bra, he realized. How did the thing fasten? He slid his hands down her rib cage and up beneath the hem.

Her mouth clung to his as she released him and got up. Protest died in his throat when she took his hands in hers. "Let's go a little mad," she murmured, her low, sexy invitation as irresistible as anything he had ever heard.

He'd be a raving lunatic if he didn't have her soon. This was madness at its finest.

If she was going for distraction because he had been left behind tonight, it was working big time.

The realization that she would do that was humbling, but it also troubled him. Compensation for missing out on the mission was not what he wanted from her. Neither was he up for fireworks celebrating a slight improvement in his sight. He stopped her halfway down the hall with a tug on her hand. "If this is medicinal or congratulatory sex, forget it."

She laughed softly. "Shut up, Will. I don't know what it is, but it's definitely not that. I want to, that's all." She stood on tiptoe and kissed his chin, which was about as high as she could reach.

"Now that I can see?" he asked, kicking himself even as the words left his mouth.

She stilled, then pulled away. "You brought that up before—your vision. That's what you really think of me?"

"No, no I don't," he admitted, shaking his head sharply and running his hand over his face. "Of course I don't. It was a knee-jerk, self-centered reaction and I'm sorry."

"You should be." A tense silence fell as they stood

there. Finally, she spoke. "I think we've said enough. I know I have. Made a perfect fool of myself."

"No, you didn't. You know I want you, too. You've got to know *that* if you don't know anything else." He might as well tell her the rest while he was at it. "But I need more, Holly. More of you than casual—"

She quickly brushed past him and headed back to the kitchen, effectively cutting off his sentence. He followed, wishing he could explain better. He tried again. "Look, I'm not demanding anything."

"Yes, you are!" she accused. "You demand everything you see and want, Will. And expect the demand to get you exactly that. You always have."

"What do you mean by that?"

"I mean ponies, bikes, cheerleaders, Harvard, whatever! Ask and ye shall receive, huh? Nothing denied you because it's your absolute due as one of the chosen few! Well, wake up, preppy. Some of us stop and think before we grab for everything that looks enticing. It's not always good for you."

He could not believe this. "Good Lord. You're a snob," he said, still disbelieving.

"Me? *I'm* the snob? Why, you self-indulgent, Gucci-shod prick!" Now she was losing it. What was that he had decided about inventive invective deserting her when she went ballistic?

"I'm wearing mud-stained sneakers in case you didn't notice."

"Not by choice!"

He could tell she was hopping mad by the jerky way she moved, shifting from one foot to the other, making him dizzy as he tried to hold a clear image.

The last thing he wanted was to upset her, but this had taken a sharp turn he hadn't expected. His fault.

He should have kept his big mouth shut and made love to her, whatever her reasons.

If he could only calm her down long enough to listen, maybe he could smooth things out. He held out his hands, palms facing her, a gesture meant to cry peace. "Okay. Stop right there before we say more that we really don't mean. Things that aren't even relevant."

"What things?" she almost shouted. "Go ahead! Say what you want to say!"

Will shut his eyes and took a deep breath, determined to sound reasonable. He propped his hands on his hips to keep from reaching for her. "Look, I can't help that I grew up with privileges you were denied. You've had to work hard to get where you are, and I know that."

She scoffed. "I had to work to *eat*, Will. From the time I was nine I rode the bus to another *world* across town and helped my mother clean houses for people like you so she would have the energy left to work her second job. Can you even imagine that? Have you ever been hungry?"

"No, Holly, not the way you mean. But I have been hungry for the things you *did* have."

"Like what? Rats for pets?" Her voice had climbed a whole octave.

"Your mother, for one thing. The way she loved you. I hear the way you talk about her. She worshiped you. She convinced you that you could be anything you set out to be because she believed that right down to her soul. Do you realize *just* how priceless that was?"

Holly sighed, clicking her tongue with obvious impatience. "Yeah, of course I know that." She dragged out the nearest chair and slumped down in it as if she were suddenly exhausted. "Poor little rich kids, you and Matt. My heart bleeds."

Her attempt at sarcasm should have made him angry, but Will knew that deep down she really meant what she said. But he didn't want her sympathy, just her understanding. She had his in spades. She'd had it rough. She'd overcome.

Will sat down across from her, leaning forward with his hands spread out in front of him, trying his best to see her face, her expression, as he spoke. "I envy you, Holly," he said quietly, honestly.

"You what?"

"You should have had an easier childhood and a free ride through college, but the hardships have made you who you are."

He cleared his throat, a little embarrassed at revealing so much, but he couldn't seem to stop. "There's no one I admire more than you, Holly. And I think I might be…"

"What?" she said, the word a mere breath of sound.

"In love with you," he admitted reluctantly.

Chapter 12

"In love with me?"

Holly almost fell out of her chair. Words promptly deserted her. He *loved* her? No way.

His steel-gray eyes, narrowed now with his effort to see, held hers like an industrial strength magnet. She was so glad there was a table between them, preventing that compelling force from slamming them together.

She buried her face in her hands, trying to think, to block out the sight of him sitting there looking so earnest and sincere, so unafraid.

As for her, she was terrified.

He couldn't *love* her. All this time they had worked together, joked in the office, clinked beer glasses at Christa's Pub, divvied up a dangerous op like kids with a bar of candy. *Here, you take that half and this part's mine.*

She was comfortable with all that and knew Will

was, too. But love? He obviously didn't know what he was saying.

She didn't want to explore any further what his words made her feel. Something like a mushroom cloud of hope kept rising and expanding inside her with the speed of light, blocking out all reason.

Her lips clamped shut to hold back words that had no business escaping.

The phone rang.

Desperate for any diversion, she jumped up, hurried past him and snatched up the handset. "Amberson."

Will almost felt relieved that Holly hadn't had a chance to reply to his little declaration. Whatever she might have said would not have a positive slant after that verbal battle they had just had. It seemed he had struck her speechless, and that was a first.

He didn't hold out much hope that she felt anything more for him than she had indicated before. Maybe it was best that way, at least for her.

"Yes, Colonel Arbin, everyone's on it. They're set up to intercept if a Stinger's fired," she was saying on the phone. "Forces should be arriving anytime now." She paused, then exclaimed, "What?"

She grabbed Will's arm and urged him closer, tilting the phone so that he could hear, too.

"Turkel and his crew have moved again," the voice said. Will tried to compare it to the one he'd heard at the river, but it was hard to tell over the phone. Southern, but not quite the same, a bit more clipped. Or possibly just urgent.

Will listened closely as the man gave the new address. "It's an old antebellum off Blaketon Road." He rattled off directions to reach it. "I can see them from where I'm concealed. They're ready with that missile. I have to stop this. There are four of them including Turkel. I think I can take 'em, but I could use one more gun.''

"The missile will be intercepted, Colonel. Don't do anything yet. You'll have backup within the next fifteen to twenty minutes,'' Holly promised. "I'll come myself.''

"Good, but hurry and get out here,'' he demanded. "And for God's sake, keep it quiet when you do. These fools are half-drunk and liable to do anything.'' The connection abruptly broke.

"It's a setup. I smell it,'' Holly said. "If he thinks he could take them down, why hasn't he done it before now? He's been trailing them for days.''

"He's got some private agenda,'' Will agreed. "But he sounds desperate to prevent that firing. At least we have that in common. Did the voice sound the same to you? Like the one at the river?''

"I think it was. Don't you?''

"Could be. You know where Blaketon Road is?'' Will asked as Holly punched in the code to contact Jack and the team.

"Yes, we passed it when we were out earlier. The exit's only a couple of miles from here.''

She turned her attention to the phone and quickly explained to Mercier the latest development according to Arbin. It was a short conversation.

"Everyone's converged at the other place out near Decatur. They're on the way, but I can reach Arbin's location long before they can,'' she told Will. "I have to go.''

"Did they leave any equipment?''

"Everything but what they're using is right here.''

He could hear her going through the stuff. "Grab an H&K and a couple of pistols, some com gear and the vests. I'll load the weapons while you suit up."

"You're staying here," she ordered, shaking her head vehemently.

"Like hell I am." He was not about to let Holly go anywhere without some kind of backup. "I can shoot at shadows if nothing else. Provide cover if you need it."

"Arbin says there are only four."

"If he is Odin, he makes five, Holly. If he's not, we might have a wild card out there somewhere."

"I know that," she told him. "I can handle it."

Will knew she could, but this was his fight even more than hers. "I don't know what's going on with Arbin, but I might be able to determine that when we get closer. What if I can tune in to something helpful? You know you need me, Holly, for that if nothing else," he said.

"No time to argue," she grumbled as she shoved a Kevlar vest into his hands. "Put this thing on then. Here's a jacket, too. But you're staying in the car!"

Fat chance of that. A target might still be blurry, but he could damn well see the bull's-eye now if the light was good. "Don't forget the flares," he said, "and the headsets."

The old mansion looked pretty spooky in the moon-light, Odin thought as he watched Turkel and the others fiddle with the launcher. Half the roof and part of the upper walls were missing along the side, and he could see them clearly from his vantage point outside. Hear them, too. They joked among themselves in their own language.

He had obtained the illegal automatics and missiles, sold them to Turkel and given the men instructions on how to load and fire the Stingers. Their one firing had been successful, if a little anticlimactic. Only three casualties.

They thought he was joining them tonight in case there were problems, but as soon as the next missile was launched, he would eliminate them all.

He would be the one who saved the day and prevented a further disaster. The one unused missile and launcher plus four dead terrorists would attest to that.

His scapegoat was in place now, too. The call was made. Everything was set.

If he had timed this all just right, the cavalry should arrive shortly after the terrorists lay dead beside the actual smoking gun.

He smiled, imagining how he, as the singular hero, could write his own ticket after that. He could expect a solid position of power and importance as an advisor in the new administration, or at the very last, a ludicrously profitable book deal.

He had planned his success down to the letter. A phone call to the press had assured that. With his identity revealed to the world within the next few hours, he would be free to accept whatever accolades were offered.

What an omen that Amberson herself had answered his last call at the number Mercier had instructed him to use. Odin had not been able to get to her since finding out that she and Griffin had survived.

She could never prove she'd seen him in the hospital, even if she thought she recognized him when she saw him next, but he had not wanted her to raise any questions. Better to be safe than sorry.

Same with Will Griffin, since he might possibly have gotten a glimpse at the airport.

How fortunate that they had left Amberson in charge here on the south side while every available resource that law enforcement and the government could muster were tripping all over each other at the abandoned site called in to Mercier earlier.

Odin congratulated himself on knowing precisely where Amberson was even if he couldn't get to her. Easy enough to determine HSA's little hideaway by checking local government transactions involving real estate and equipment. Did they think he didn't know how these places were set up and who kept track of them?

They had trained him to uncover deeper, darker secrets than something like that.

Amberson would come out here first, and he could get rid of her and whatever skeleton crew she brought with her before the main forces arrived.

There would be time to find and deal with Griffin later. According to his father, Will Griffin still hadn't regained his sight, so the threat of identification by him was negligible for the time being.

Odin checked the time, antsy to act. Air traffic would probably be halted by now. If the helicopter didn't fly over in time, he would have to go ahead and kill Turkel's bunch and leave both the Stingers intact.

That would also be effective, but another air disaster sure would emphasize future vulnerabilities, not to mention inflate everyone's patriotism and punch up his hero factor.

Holly tapped number one on the speed dial and handed Will the phone the minute they were settled in the car. "Get an ETA from Jack. I doubt they'll use choppers because of the missiles."

Hopefully all incoming and outgoing air traffic would be grounded by now and she wouldn't have to worry about missiles. She ran through possible scenarios. Arbin might be lying in wait for her, so she would probably have to deal with him first.

If there were any aircraft in the area, she hoped to heaven the new interceptor ground-to-air missile system the Army brought in could stop the Stinger. The old GTAs were notoriously inconsistent, despite all the good press they had gotten in the war.

Will had completed his call. "Jack says they'll be there in about half an hour, thirty-five minutes tops. How do you want to play this?"

"Stealth's the only way, so you'll have to stay back, Will," she told him. "You might be able to help once I get there, but leading you in would slow me down too much."

"So stay out of your way," he said.

"That's about it. I can do this. You've always trusted me before."

"I trust you now," he declared. "I just wish I were going with you."

He was using his head now and she wouldn't have to worry about him throwing himself in the line of fire. "Check your brain waves, will you? I'd sure like to know what Arbin's up to."

"I'm getting nothing from him so far," he admitted after a few minutes. "Dead quiet."

She took the Blaketon exit and checked her odometer. Traffic was heavy. She wove in and out, zipped into the right lane after they had gone about three miles, and watched for a turnoff at four. There it was.

The road was four-lane and busy, lined with subdivisions and strip malls. "Right in the middle of civilization. You'd think these bozos would choose somewhere isolated."

"Maybe they think it'll be easier to disappear in a crowd," he said.

"Here we go," she muttered, turning left when she saw the sign Arbin had described. "This is more like it. Hills and trees, not that many houses."

Will had fallen silent. She risked a glance. He was staring straight ahead, his mouth slightly open. "He's outside. It's…old. The roof's gone." After a few seconds, he shuddered as if coming awake after a bad dream. "They're there."

"Turkel?" she asked softly, not wanting to break his concentration, but unable to keep from prompting him.

"Oh, God!" he gasped suddenly, then shook his head violently. He pressed the thumb-size speaker closer to mouth. "Jack. It's up. I repeat, the missile is up! Do you copy?"

Holly watched the sky as she sped down the road. A streak zipped through the moonlight dead ahead. "I have a visual!" She lost sight of it before the words were out. Seconds ticked by, then they heard the explosion.

"The interceptor got it?" Holly asked.

"Can't tell from the sound." He pressed the button on his mike again. "Jack, come in." He tried several more times without success. "Interference."

He pulled out the cellphone and felt for the speed dial. It rang and Mercier answered. "What's up?"

"The SAM. Did you see it?"

"Heard the boom and saw the flash. No word yet on what it hit. Where are you?"

"Close. We'll cut contact now until something breaks," Will told him.

"Roger that. We're on the way."

Will put the phone away and spoke to Holly. "I'm switching the mike to short range. How's yours working?"

Holly adjusted her headset. "I read you fine, but don't transmit to me unless you have to, and if you do, use clicks."

"I *know* the drill," he snapped, knowing full well she was so hyped she barely knew he was there.

Holly had wheeled off the road, driving a crow's flight route toward where she figured the missile had been launched.

The Jeep bumped over a field and came to a stop when a long stand of pines blocked the way. "I'm going in," she said. She jumped out, hurriedly retrieved her weapons from the back. "Get out. It's too open here. I want you in the woods."

Will suppressed a frisson of doubt. He would be lost as a goose among a bunch of trees that blocked out what moonlight there was. He climbed out, put a hand on her shoulder, prepared to do exactly as she said, since she was now officially in charge of this.

"You might need a flare if I…I'm delayed or something." She stuck one in the pocket of his jacket. "Here's a pistol. Where do you want it?"

He took it and slid it under the waistband of his jeans in back.

"Cellphone?"

"Right here." He patted his shirt pocket.

She grabbed his hand and hurried him through the

trees for a ways, then stopped. "Here's a good spot. Have a seat and I'll be back before you know it."

She was gone without another word. Will had to bite his tongue to keep from shouting to her, warning her to be careful, rapping out cautionary phrases that he would normally never utter to a seasoned pro like Holly. All he could do was wait, hope for the best, imagine the worst and worry like hell.

At that moment, he could clearly understand why relationships in this business seldom worked out.

Holly reached the house in less than three minutes. It was closer than she had thought, a vacant monstrosity virtually surrounded by woods. Eerie, like something out of a horror movie.

She crossed the open yard and approached from the side, then stopped to calm her pulse rate. Firing while your heart was racing ninety to nothing would almost guarantee disaster, especially with several people firing back. She inhaled a breath and released it slowly.

When she felt her muscles unkink, she continued along the cracked tabby walls to the corner bordering the front. She peeped around it and saw only one guard, armed with a wicked-looking machine gun that was a whole lot larger than her H&K.

Holly knew she would have to take him out, silently if possible in order to avoid alerting the others.

She made a cat sound, a wild one, then risked another peek. He tossed down his cigarette and craned his neck in her direction. She knew he couldn't see her. She moved back when the beam of his flashlight raked the corner of the house.

Holly meowed again, then softly called, "Kitty, kitty, kitty!" in a childlike voice. She banged a fist-size rock against an old empty paint can that lay on the ground at her feet. Another peek. He was coming to investigate, probably expecting to find some kid out looking for a runaway cat. She hoped.

She placed her weapon on the ground and psyched herself up. The sound of his footsteps drew nearer and nearer, as did the flashlight beam.

The instant he rounded the corner, she caught him with a chop across his windpipe and yanked his weapon out of his hand simultaneously. He curled forward, grasping his throat.

Before he could recover his breath, she grabbed up the heavy flashlight he had dropped and conked him on the temple twice.

There was still a pulse. She snatched plastic wrist restraints out of her pocket and secured him quickly. She searched him for a blade, found it and tossed it into the woods. He wouldn't be coming around anytime soon. One down.

Again she steadied her breathing before doing a toe-heel creep to the front door. It was open. She slid inside like an invisible wraith.

Haunting Tara, she thought as she looked around the spacious entrance hall. There were no lights except those coming from the upper floor.

She heard laughter and scraping sounds, as if the guys upstairs were getting things together. Yep, they would have been wise to scram the second after that missile took off. What were they thinking?

She bounded toward the stairs and up to the second floor, where she stopped and assessed. A door down the hall stood open.

Silently she crept to one side of it. She could feel the draft from the missing roof. The cacophony of several men speaking Arabic indicated they were occupied in some kind of argument.

Two soft clicks sounded in her earpiece. *Not now, Will!* Boy, she would give her eyeteeth to have him beside her right now, but not clicking in her ear from a distance.

She inhaled, exhaled, got herself together for the big show. This was it! She whirled into the doorway and opened fire. No warning, no identification. So let 'em sue her.

Three fell immediately, but one had crawled behind a broken bedstead. He was holding the shoulder-fired Stinger launcher upright while he rattled off a desperate threat in his own language.

The words were unintelligible, but his message was clear enough. He would fire the thing if she didn't do something. But what could she do? If she fired, so would he. *Standoff.*

She knew the drill. No rule held hard and fast in a situation like this.

So, analyze what he's thinking, what his options are, which one he's most likely to choose. Her gaze holding his, Holly studied his wide, dark eyes. She didn't see them as the eyes of a zealot. Too frightened.

Would he fire it anyway, go out in a blaze of glory in hopes of reward in the next life? Maybe not, since he hadn't yet. She figured this man wasn't quite that ready to die. Maybe she could deal.

Normally it took two to fire the Stingers, but one could do it if he was determined enough. Holly was fairly certain there were no planes in the air overhead right now, but who knew where this thing would land if he fired it?

The man left had no other weapon handy that she

could see. He wore a snug knit shirt and his pants were too tight to conceal anything.

Holly held up her hands, made her voice as calming as she could. "All right, all right! See? Look at me now. I'm laying down."

She crouched, slowly placed the H&K on the floor, stood and made a placating gesture with her empty hands.

"Put that down very slowly and get out of here," she said, motioning for him to scram, enunciating each word. "You can go."

It would be child's play to chase him down once he did. She could catch him before he got out of the house.

The second she decided he was about to lower the launcher, she heard a dull thud. A hole appeared between the man's eyes and he crumpled to the floor.

Not her shot. Holly hit the deck. She grabbed up the machine gun and scrambled behind a ragged, over-stuffed chair.

The missile had fallen on top of the terrorist and bounced, rolling harmlessly to one side. Holly hoped the thing wouldn't go off by itself.

In the meantime, there was another shooter in the room with a silenced weapon. Where the hell was he? "Show yourself or I'll make this place a colander!" she shouted.

"I'm Colonel Lex Arbin, former Military Intelligence. Hold your fire!"

"Where are you, Colonel?"

"In here, behind this door. I'm opening it and coming out."

So that's where he was hiding. Was it a closet? "Holster your weapon or I *will* open fire. Keep your hands above your head," she warned him.

A door to her left opened and he stepped out. "Who're you with?"

"Agent Amberson, HSA Special Ops."

"There's one more outside somewhere."

"I got him coming in."

He sighed and began to lower his hands. "I was concealed, waiting for Odin to show up. They were expecting him."

"Keep your hands up," she warned. "I want you just like that when company gets here."

"Look, honey, I'm real tired. I've hardly had any sleep in the past week and a half chasing these jerks around. Shoot me if you want to, but this is absurd!" His hands drifted down.

Holly fired a burst, missing his foot by inches. His hands flew up. "Very good, *honey,*" she crooned, then read him his rights.

He listened impatiently. "Jeez, woman, I'm on your side."

"We'll see. It could be that Odin's a lot closer than you'd like me to believe."

"Don't be ridiculous. I'm the one who clued y'all in on this mess. You saw I stopped him from firing that missile."

"Yeah, but you sort of let those first two slide right by, didn't you. Three innocent people are dead because you failed to stop that first one. God knows how many if that second one hit."

"Two went down to Macon. I kept watch on the larger group. I thought all the missiles were still here."

"Why didn't you notify someone to go after the other two? Tell us where they went?" she demanded.

"I didn't know where they were going!" he insisted. "I called in every chance I got. The CIA has been two steps behind me all the way. I've been in constant touch.''

"CIA?'' Holly doubted that. Clay had been with the Company. They would have called Sextant the minute something like this turned up. ''Who's your contact?''

''Like I could tell you that.''

''And tonight's firing? Why didn't you step in? You're pretty well armed. With that silencer, you could have dropped them all before they knew what hit 'em.''

''Odin was supposed to show up, they said. He was the brains of the outfit, so I figured they'd wait for him. I was assured the authorities would ground everything anyway.''

He looked nervous and his back was to the open door. If that wasn't a closet and there was another exit through there, Holly feared he might simply step back and disappear before she could fire if she didn't remain vigilant. She reminded herself that this guy was former Intelligence. He probably had the same training she did, and that's what she would try.

Suddenly, two shots popped from somewhere to her right. Arbin grabbed his chest and fell. Holly dropped to her knees and scrambled backward to the hall door.

Damn! She hadn't had a chance to check the other three men for signs of life after her initial intrusion. One of them had obviously survived.

And then something whistled through the open roof.

Will knew help was at least a quarter hour away, maybe more. Suddenly, like an out-of-control brushfire, Odin's euphoric sense of power flooded through his mind.

Staccato bursts of fully automatics popped like multiple strands of firecrackers. Will couldn't tell if the sounds were in his head or if he actually heard them. Unless he deliberately broke the connection with Odin, he wouldn't know.

A long silence ensued. Will felt incredible tension, a sense of urgency. Excitement. In his mind he could see the end of a weapon of some kind. Not a Stinger, but something round, olive-drab.

Then an enormous boom and blast of heat shook him. No, it shook Odin. A grenade? Had he launched a grenade?

Where was Holly? Will pushed the mike to his lips and clicked frantically. No answer. Changed to long-range frequency and again pressed it. ''Sextant? Come in!''

He yanked the cell out of his pocket, then stuffed it back in. What was the use? They'd be here as soon as humanly possible anyway, whether he called or not.

Somebody had to do something here, and there was nobody but the blind guy.

He had to get to Holly. Somehow help her. Trusting that she could handle herself was one thing, but loving her was something else.

His eyes were adjusting a little, still insisting on tunnel vision. Very bad tunnel vision, at that, but he could see slivers of light flickering between the thin trunks of the trees. At least he was going in the right direction.

Battling through the thick underbrush, he emerged in a yard. The grass under his feet made for easier walking, and the fire from the house lit his way.

Will squinted at the old house and could see flames engulfing the top floor. ''Holly?'' he called.

Scanning the scene was like looking through a camera with the split aperture center only half focused. He thanked God he could see that little bit.

If Holly was inside that firetrap, he had to get her out *now*. Will ran as fast as he dared, praying he wouldn't trip over anything that would slow him down.

No more gunfire erupted. No sounds broke the night other than the roar and crackle of the blaze. The front door stood wide open.

He quickly slid inside, weapon ready, hoping his eyes would adjust.

It was too dark to see anything at all. If she was below that conflagration on the top floor, she would answer. If she wasn't, he didn't much care what happened to him.

"Holly!" he shouted as loudly as possible. "Holly, are you in here?"

"Will!" she answered immediately. "Get out!"

"Where are you?" he demanded, straining to see in the darkness. *Nothing.*

"Second floor landing. I'm crawling down now. I can make it. Get *out* of here!"

"Are you hurt?" he called, following the sound of her voice. He bumped into the stair rail and grabbed on to it, taking the stairs two at a time. "Answer me!"

"Yeah," she said, grabbing his ankle when he reached the landing. "I think my leg's busted."

Will stuffed the gun back in his belt and reached down to lift her. "Fireman's carry," he warned. "Hang on. I won't drop you."

He positioned her over his right shoulder, hooked one arm around the backs of her knees and grabbed the railing with his left hand.

Carefully and quickly, he descended with her and felt his way outside. He heard the first floor collapse inside just as they exited.

Exhausted and coughing, he deposited her on the

ground as far away from the house as he could carry her. Frantically he ran his hands over her head, shoulders and chest, checking for burns or wounds.

Her hair was singed. He could smell it. Her shirt was ripped at the shoulder.

Sliding his fingers carefully along her ribs beneath her heavy shirt, he progressed to her waist and hips. She had lost her weapons and headset.

Again his mind flooded with a euphoria that felt manic, evil. As if from a short distance away, he suddenly pictured himself and Holly sprawled there on the grass.

He tensed the same second she grasped his arm, her fingers biting into his muscle.

"Will," she said, her voice deadly quiet with warning.

She didn't need to define the problem. He knew who it was.

Chapter 13

"Playing blindman's bluff, Griffin?" The deep voice, somehow familiar, taunted him. *Odin.*

"He's armed," Holly muttered.

"And dangerous," Odin added with a chuckle, striding forward so that he stood between them and the burning house, a menacing black shadow. Harbinger of death. "Though I did take a bullet," he added, sounding proud of it.

"Probably your own," Holly said with a snort.

"Who's going to know? As soon as I shoot you and Griffin, I'll toss this weapon in the front door. That place will be an ash heap in no time. They'll find the three of us out here in the yard. You two dead, and me unconscious from my shoulder wound." He laughed. "All the villains and their toys inside, burning to a crisp, but they'll be identifiable enough for my purposes."

"And what would those purposes be? Why in the world are you doing this?" Holly demanded.

"Glory and reward, sweetheart. But I don't mind sharing the renown a little. I'll explain how you blundered in there with a blind man, got me shot and screwed my chance to prevent Turkel from firing the Stinger. We'll all be famous."

"Infamous," Will corrected. He felt Holly's fingers easing the Glock from the back of his belt, so he played for time and gathered what info he could. This was not likely to end with a prisoner to question. "Why give up the whole shipment of Stingers at the airport? Why keep only three?"

"Ah well, I'm not a monster. I never had any intention of using more, so I stored my little cache somewhere else. Those three seemed enough to rally outrage and patriotism again. Bring us together, so to speak."

Will fought the urge to lunge at the man and choke the life out of him. "Who the hell do you think you are, anyway, some kind of god? Who are you really?"

"Don't you know me, William? Your own beloved godfather?"

Will barely controlled his shock. "Jim Fielding?"

"James *Odin* Fielding, one and the same. I couldn't resist using the middle name Mother saddled me with, since it seemed so appropriate, a god both benevolent and merciless."

Will had not seen the man, a friend of his father's, since high school graduation. "I guess you sort of slacked off on the job," he commented. "Not to mention that you killed your other godson. Why, Jim?"

"You both knew me. You were a threat. Neither of you would have understood why I'm doing this."

"Did you know we'd be at the airport that night?"

"I had a word with Matt's AIC. It was my idea to request you since you and Matt worked so well together before."

"And Arbin? How did he fit in?" Holly asked.

"The good colonel played right into my hands, arranging everything while I fed him information and gave him good advice."

"You've been running Arbin all this time?"

"Absolutely. He had no idea I was the Odin he was supposed to be after, but he and I had worked together before when he was on active duty. He trusted me to advise him and keep him informed, while he obligingly did the surveillance work."

"What a mistake that was," Holly scoffed.

Fielding smiled. "Arbin turned out to be the perfect patsy, bless his heart. He'll make a fine Odin substitute, don't you think? However, I did regret having to shoot you two that night, Will," he said with patently fake contrition. "I knew all about Matt's little psychic gift, you see. He made me a believer very early on. Who knows what he might have sensed? And you, Will, do you have it, too?"

"In spades," he told him, biting off the words. "I got right inside your sick mind, you son of a bitch."

"Ah, such language! But you didn't realize who I was, after all, did you? I can't tell you what a relief that was."

Now Will knew why the man's voice had sounded so familiar. Though they'd had only a few conversations when he and Matt were growing up, Jim Fielding had been born and raised in the same area as their dad, had been educated with him and had the exact same accent.

Will couldn't see his godfather clearly now, backlit

as he was by the fire, but he recalled what Fielding looked like. Physically fit, dark hair, deep-set eyes and bushy brows. A clotheshorse.

He drank Scotch, Will remembered. Swilled it down like water. Matt had joked about getting their alky godparent to introduce them to the gods of booze. Too bad Fielding wasn't soused now. He sounded stone-cold sober. "It *has* been a few years. I'd almost forgotten you existed," Will said.

"I'm afraid the Company has kept me pretty busy," Fielding explained.

"You're CIA?" Will was not all that surprised.

"Just like your dear old dad."

Now Will was not only surprised, but positively shocked, though he managed not to show it.

Suddenly all his parents' frequent absences made sense.

So did their refusal to discuss much about their freewheeling lifestyle and why they had always distanced themselves from the twins and their extended families. Even the posting as attaché to the embassy in Italy fell into place.

"Are you saying my father's in on all of this?" Will had to know.

Fielding laughed. "Hardly. But he will be, after the fact. I'm certain he'll be happy to use his influence to get me a prime position once he hears about my heroics tonight. I could always depend on old Matthew, Senior, to do the right thing."

Will felt a surge of relief that his father wasn't involved.

He knew Holly had his pistol now. He had to draw the bead on himself, in case Fielding was aiming at her. She needed a chance to get off a shot.

"Oh, God, I'm going to be sick," Will groaned.

He sat up, doubled over slowly and groaned again, listing forward and to his right, away from Holly. He clutched his stomach. As he curled, he felt the flare gun in his pocket. Slowly he pulled it out, keeping it hidden with his body.

"I'll put you out of your misery, don't worry," Fielding assured him. "Just so you know I'm not a bad godfather after all, go ahead and say your prayers. Time is running short and I really should—"

Will jerked up the hidden flare gun and fired at Fielding's shape.

Holly's ears rang. Her hands were numb on the pistol after firing six rounds. "Will, are you all right?" she asked.

"I'm good. You weren't hit, were you?"

"Nope, his shots went wild, thanks to you. I'm just a little shook up. I'll be back in a second."

She crawled the dozen feet or so over to Odin's body, her leg aching like crazy. The noxious stench of the flare searing through the fiber of the protective vest Odin wore, combined with burned flesh, made her nauseous. He had also taken a few rounds from her Glock. Though he was clearly dead, Holly automatically leaned over and checked for a pulse. Then she crawled back beside Will and collapsed on the grass.

"Is he dead?" he asked.

"Oh yeah."

"What about the others? In the house?"

"One guard secured over there in the side yard. The rest, including Arbin, were upstairs."

She looked at the flames devouring the building she

had escaped, then surveyed the lower floor and surrounding grounds.

Something moved, snaking its way from the front door.

''Will! Someone else made it out of the house!'' How long had he been there? ''Help me get up!''

He pushed himself up, then grabbed her hand and helped tug her to her feet. She put weight on her bad leg and found she could stand, though it hurt like hell. She leaned on Will and limped, telling him which way to go.

She had the Glock ready as they slowly approached the prone figure, now facedown and unmoving. When they got close, she could see by the clothing who it was.

''It's Arbin! Help me get him farther away from the fire. Here are his arms. I'll take him by the feet and lead, okay?''

''I've got him. You go ahead of us and we'll let his feet drag. Can you walk by yourself?''

''If we take it slow.''

Will struggled to get a better grip. ''Hop if you have to, but let's hurry and get away from here.'' Smoke was pouring through the open door, flames licking out the lower windows, the heat ferocious.

Holly led the way as Will hauled the colonel to the far side of the yard where they had been before, next to the trees and upwind of the smoke.

''How bad's…he hurt?'' Will asked, coughing deeply between words.

''Let me see,'' she ordered, ripping the flashlight from her belt loop and directing the beam.

She examined the colonel. ''Two entry wounds, one near the top of his shoulder that's exited. Seems superficial. The other's under his arm and missed his vest by not more than an inch. Rapid pulse. Unconscious. How in the world did he get out of there? The upstairs was an inferno. I don't see how anyone could have survived that.''

She had seen Arbin take a hit just before the explosion. The blast had knocked her clear of the doorway, but the door itself had blocked the worst of it for her. Still, she had landed against the opposite wall of the hallway and somehow banged her leg against something. Her crawl to the stairs had been painful and slow as fire roared through the roofless section she had just left.

''No way I could have gone back in,'' she told herself out loud, feeling guilty that she had left the man for dead. While trying to figure out how he had managed to save himself, she yanked off her long-sleeved shirt and was padding Ardin's wound with it.

''Where the heck *is* everybody? They should be here by now,'' she muttered.

She felt chilled wearing only her sleeveless tank top. Chilled right down to her soul, and jumpy. Her nerves were right there on the edge. How close she had come to dying, not once but twice tonight. And both times, Will had saved her. What were the odds?

She realized he had been feeling around on the ground and located his discarded headset with the attached mike. He pressed it to talk. ''Jack? Will. You read me?''

''Thank God!'' Mercier's voice boomed, even with the volume turned down. ''Status?''

''Mission accomplished. All the eggs in the basket. We need an ambulance for Arbin. The snakes are all dead but one.''

"We're two minutes away, strung out like a damn parade. Fire trucks, ambulances and everything in the state with a badge. Is Holly all right?"

Will smiled at her. "Better than fine."

"Great. I'm turning off Blaketon now."

In less than a minute the yard filled with vehicles. The first ambulance headed straight for them, stopping only a few yards away. The paramedics quickly stabilized Arbin and loaded him in the back.

"Are you all right, ma'am? Sir?"

"Get him to the hospital or you're gonna lose him," Holly told the paramedic. "We can wait." They watched the ambulance pull away.

Will laid down the headset. "I'm going to kiss you senseless now because I'm so damn glad you're alive."

"Yeah, me, too!" Holly threw her arms around his neck and kissed him hard. She couldn't afford to make it last the way she wanted to. They had to hurry. The yard teemed with official vehicles and personnel, but she needed this kiss more than anything.

She needed *him* more than anything, this man who had saved her life repeatedly and trusted her ability to do the same for him. He needed her, too, whether he was ready to admit it or not.

His mouth ate at hers as if he were starving for it. Reluctantly Holly pushed away, giving his Kevlar-covered chest a couple of firm, reassuring pats. This definitely would be continued.

"Here, help me get up," she said.

"Should you stand? I think you ought to get that leg x-rayed first."

"Can't be broken, the way I've been hopping around on it. Probably just banged up a little. I don't want to look like one of the wounded, okay?"

"All right, if you promise to lean on me." Grudgingly, he took her hands and pulled her to her feet, grasping her elbows so she could keep her weight off her leg.

The sirens finally stopped wailing. Cars were still piling down the drive, competing for places to park as the fire crews scrambled around the two trucks, preparing to contain the blaze. It seemed pretty hopeless.

"I'm not done with you, Griffin," Holly said, gazing up into his face. Never had he looked more heroic, more capable of doing anything he set his mind on.

"You can make book on that. Want to take a little R and R when we're done here, maybe run up to Schroon Lake with me and feed the loons?" he asked, matching her volume.

"Feed the loons?" she repeated, grinning. "And?"

"Open up the cabin. Chop some wood. Maybe pop a little popcorn. Finish what we started, this time without an audience?"

Tempting. She planned to take him up on it. A figure striding in their direction caught her eye. "Uh-oh. Boss is headed this way and looks like he's ready to choke us both. What'd we do?"

"We? I didn't do anything. I'm just along for the ride."

She leaned in close and stood on tiptoe, not caring who saw them getting cozy. "You hauled me out of that house. You put a flare right in the middle of Odin's chest."

"I hope the bastard's still smoking," Will said bitterly. "Damn traitor. There ought to be a special place in hell for people like him."

Holly looked over at the body on the ground, now surrounded by technicians, then back at Will. She grasped his hands in hers and held them to her. "You got him, Will."

"Now I can go see Matt," he said, glancing away. "I can say goodbye." He paused, swallowed hard, then looked down at her, his gray eyes glinting, not quite meeting hers. "Will you come with me?"

"You gotta ask? Where else would a partner be at a time like that?"

"Back to *partners* again that quickly, huh? Just like old times."

"Ah yes, the good old days. Now we have this new complication," she said, her tone wry. "You think you love me. Unless you were joking."

"And I think you love me, too. How funny is that?"

"It's nothing to laugh about," she said. He was too right.

"No joke. How close is Jack to us? Can I kiss you again?"

Someone cleared his throat noisily. "I'm too close. If you two will unlock for a few minutes, I'd like to know what the devil happened here."

Holly swiveled around, her chin raised in challenge. Jack's frowning features were flickering in the myriad strobes of the vehicle flashers. "Well?" he prompted.

"Holly needs to have her leg x-rayed," Will interjected. "It might be fractured."

"No, it's not," she assured Jack. "I'll see about it later." She hurriedly changed the topic and began to brief him. "The Stinger was fired from the top floor there." She broke off. "Was it intercepted?"

"No time, it hit a low-flying chopper from one of the local news stations. They must have gone up to investigate when they picked up radio traffic. God knows there was plenty of it on our end." He sighed heavily and shook his head. "I guess they didn't think the ban on air traffic applied to them. What happened next?"

She filled him in and then pointed to the body on the ground. "That's Odin. He was a Company man. J. O. Fielding. He'd had it with working in the background. Took a little power trip. Wanted recognition."

"Helluva way to get it." Hands clasped behind his back, Jack walked over, parted the techs who were examining Odin's body and looked down. Then he came back. "I'll put Clay on this. Find out all we can."

"I...I knew him, but not well. He was a friend of my father's," Will said. "My godfather."

Jack shared a glance with Holly, then switched his regard to Will. "I'm sorry. I'm sure your father had no idea what sort of man he was."

"I hope not. Fielding said not. Still, I know you'll have to check that out."

Suddenly his gaze narrowed on Jack, as if something significant occurred to him. "You *knew* my father was CIA?"

"Yes," his boss admitted.

"All this time. But no one saw fit to tell me," Will said evenly. Holly knew exactly who he meant by that.

"*Need to know* rules applied," Jack reminded him. "He was in deep cover."

Again Jack looked at Holly with a wince of regret. Obviously Will had deduced that if Jack knew about his dad, she did, too.

She had been the one who had done Will's background investigation before Jack had hired him, and she was thorough. Even though Matthew Griffin, Senior, worked under deep cover, and his records were not supposed to be available to anyone checking, Sextant had total access.

"So I'll be on suspension until this is cleared," Will guessed.

"No, you're on medical leave until your eyes improve," Jack told him. "Then I'll expect you back on the job, regardless of how the investigation goes."

Will's lips pressed tightly together as his strong jaw clenched. He turned toward the burning house and walked some distance away from where Holly stood with Jack.

Eric came dashing between the vehicles to join Will. The questions started immediately. It looked to Holly as if his debriefing was beginning on site.

"I'll have Eric take Will back to the safe house for the rest of the night. He'll be flying home first thing in the morning," Mercier said.

"Not alone!" Holly exclaimed. She had been with him almost constantly since the shooting. She wouldn't relax for a second if he were out of her sight now.

Jack's frown deepened. "He will hardly be alone, Holly."

She swallowed her pride. "I need to be with him, Jack," she admitted, glancing over to where Eric and Will were deep in conversation.

"I know," he said with a nod, "but this mission takes precedence over anything personal, Holly. We'll have to iron out jurisdictional issues, go over the debris when the ashes cool, take statements from Arbin and the other survivor, get the bodies identified, and prepare to follow up if these attacks are part of something larger and more organized than we now know about." He stopped to take a breath.

"But you have Clay and Eric!" She glanced around

the crowded yard. "Plus everybody else and his uncle!"

"And you, too, whether you like it or not. You know I can't let you go. You were central to bringing this down."

"So was Will," she argued. "He did just as much as I did. Let him stay, too."

"Only long enough to make his report. That shouldn't take more than a couple of hours. Don't argue with me, Holly. If you do, I can only think your work is taking second place."

"Maybe it is!" she snapped. "Yes, I *know* it is. So go ahead and fire me!"

Jack shook his head wearily and expelled a harsh breath. Then he grasped her upper arms and gave her a little shake. "Listen to yourself. You're still pumped from all the excitement and close calls. You're not thinking straight. Pull yourself together, Amberson."

Holly took a deep breath, appalled at what she had just said. "I…I didn't mean to lose it. Give me a minute." She ran a hand over her eyes, covering them for a moment to regain her composure.

Okay, Will did come first, before anything; she had to admit that. But she had taken an oath and had a responsibility she couldn't drop the second it became inconvenient for her personal needs. She loved Will more, but she loved her job, too. What was she thinking, jeopardizing it this way?

She moved her hand away and gave her head a shake, as if that would rattle the marbles back into place. It didn't help much, but she tried to look halfway sane when she met Jack's gaze.

"That's better," he said. "Will's mad as hell because we never told him about his father. He's mad at *you*. Do you understand that?''

"I couldn't tell him, any more than you could have. Surely he understands that." But Holly had seen his expression. Jack was right. Will was mad.

"He'll get over it, I'm sure, but he needs some time to digest all that's happened and to cool off a little. You have to let him go. You know that, Holly."

"Yeah," she said dispiritedly, "I know."

"Give it a week," Jack told her. "We should wrap up the bulk of this by then. Soon as we do that, you can courier what we have to the director in D.C., then go and see how Will's doing. Agreed?"

"Agreed." Holly figured it would be the longest week of her life. "But you'll have to get the others to do the legwork."

Jack just smiled.

She looked for Will again, but he and Eric had disappeared into the chaos surrounding them.

Jack would expect her to stay here with him at the crime scene most of the night, and she wouldn't even be able to tell Will goodbye.

Just as well. That would sound too final, anyway. If she raced after him now and spoke to him in his current mood, it might actually *be* final.

In the distance, she caught sight of the top of his head and Eric's above several of the unmarked cars. "See you," she whispered, then looked away.

Jack threw an arm around her shoulders, giving her a comforting squeeze. "Come on, lean on me. Let's go find a medic and see about that leg. Maybe somebody's got hot coffee with a load of caffeine. I think you might be experiencing a little shock."

Definitely shock, no question about that. She hadn't

realized until tonight just how deeply she loved Will. And she had been so right to worry about doing that. It was affecting the job already.

What if he never forgave her for not explaining about his father? What would he think if he ever learned that his mother worked for the Company, too, and that Holly knew that as well?

That knowledge might have helped alleviate much of his bitterness about his parents' neglect of him and his brother over the years. As far as Holly was concerned, that was no excuse at all for abandoning their children, but Will might see it differently and think she could have saved him some grief if she had shared the information.

Surely after he calmed down and thought about it, Will would realize she'd had no choice about whether to tell him. His parents worked deep cover. Holly knew she had no reason to feel guilty, but she did.

Even if he had the whole story and forgave her completely, they would still have the problem of working together to deal with.

How could they ever partner up again if they were each more worried about the other than about the mission they were responsible for?

That would mean she'd soon have to make a choice she didn't even want to think about. She still might end up without either Will or this position with Sextant if she didn't pull herself together, make a firm decision immediately and stick to her guns.

She should be reveling in the success of the mission right about now, doing mental high fives that they had wiped out a nest of terrorists and brought down a traitor. But Holly had never felt so low. So lost.

A little caffeine and an Ace bandage were not going to help.

Chapter 14

Alone, Will left the visitors' center at Arlington National Cemetery, map in hand. He studied it briefly, then set out on the long walk to find Matt's grave.

There were others strolling among the sea of white markers, and paying tribute, but they were few and not nearby. The weather had turned cold. Occasional fluffy snowflakes drifted down, melting now but promising a blanket of white. Mid-December was not a prime time for sightseers, and he was glad of that.

The two weeks following his return from Atlanta had been filled with a long, drawn-out medical evaluation, intense counseling ordered by Mercier, and a forced vacation that Will hated. He needed to work. His eyes were fine now.

Everyone from the office had come by to see him. Except Holly. He missed her, spent every night thinking about her. Remembering. But he hadn't asked about her beyond how she was doing. Fine, they said.

Said it evasively, too, which made him worry about whether she really was all right. That was a heavy body count in Atlanta. Things like that weighed on the soul, even if the deaths were necessary.

Will had endured more testing, lengthy and frustrating, that dealt with his psychic power to mind-link. Not once had they found any evidence, or even any indication, that he could still do that. He had tried, God knows, but whatever he'd had seemed to have deserted him. The so-called experts finally decided that only impending and potentially lethal danger triggered it. Privately, Will thought that his restored sense of sight must have replaced it completely. He found it a relief.

He suspected Jack's keeping him away from the office and out of the loop on any current operations did have to do with the ongoing investigation surrounding J. O. Fielding and his connection with Will's parents. A government agent turning was serious business.

Holly would be involved with the interrogations, he was sure of that. The number of people privy to the knowledge of his father's real employment would be kept to a minimum, and she already knew. They would use her talent for evaluation of the subjects questioned.

The map crinkled as his gloved hand fisted. "She should be here. With me," he mumbled to himself.

But you didn't want her. You didn't call.

Will halted. Looked around. But the voice had been in his head. His voice, but with that sardonic tone Matt had always used when taunting him.

"My imagination's running wild," he said with a short, bitter laugh.

That wouldn't be a first, but no, I'm here.

Will shook his head. He should have paid more attention when the doctors were trying to ferret out any psychoses. "I have got to stop this. He's gone," he told himself firmly.

Soon, but not yet. Keep walking.

Will resumed his pace, turning where he was supposed to, noting the numbers. Maybe coming here was not a good idea. He thought he had accepted Matt's death, his absence. Apparently he hadn't. He walked on in silence, grateful for it, yet wishing he had one last chance to speak with Matt. His mind was trying to furnish that, he guessed. Maybe he should just run with it. If you couldn't go a little crazy at your twin's grave, where should you?

"So here you are," he said with a nod as he found the marker. "One of thousands, but you were always unique except in looks."

So are you and don't forget that. Holly has always thought so.

Will smiled down at the headstone. "Yeah, I know."

You'll be okay now, bro. I promise. Long and happy life. Have a couple of children. Name the first one after me, would you?

"Matilda?"

Laughter erupted, though Will knew he was only smiling. He looked up at the sky. The snow had stopped. The sun was coming out.

This is it, Will. You're on your own. No goodbyes, okay? Go live.

"I'll be seeing you then," Will whispered as he looked down once more. His vision was blurred again, this time with tears he refused to shed.

He crouched and reached into his pocket for an old silver dollar their grandfather had given him when he and Matt were ten. He poked it deep into the ground with his finger and smoothed the soil over it. "That's for luck. You always wanted mine after you lost yours.''

Silence.

Matt was gone. Not in Will's head and not under that marker or the paltry little piece of silver. Strangely enough, Will felt good about that rather than devastated as he thought he should be. He would miss Matt's presence as long as he lived, but mourning seemed somehow wrong, not what Matt would want.

Will stood and turned to leave. ''Holly?''

''He's at peace now?'' She walked past him to Matt's marker, bent over and placed a little bunch of violets in front, then straightened to face him again. She looked beautiful, as usual. The black coat and red plaid scarf were new. Her smart little black leather shoes were wet from the slush.

''What are you doing here?'' he asked.

She smiled at him, brushing at the moisture on her cheeks with her bright red gloves. ''I promised,'' she said, clearing her throat and stepping closer. ''I always keep my promises. Friends do that.''

Will nodded, smoothing out the map, folding it and tucking it in his pocket. ''I've missed you. How's the leg?''

''Wasn't broken, just bruised. It's okay.'' She shrugged and turned to walk with him. She took his arm, probably a habit she had acquired when he'd needed her guidance, but her nearness felt so good he wasn't about to protest.

''How have you been?'' she asked. ''Jack told me your vision's much better and you'll be coming back to work soon.''

''I'm fine now. Any fallout I should know about?'' He purposely said it that way, hoping she would understand that he was good with it if she couldn't tell him anything.

"Your parents have been cleared. They're well, by the way, same as ever."

"That's considered *well?*" he asked with a short laugh to cover his lingering bitterness. He had to get rid of that, he told himself sternly. It served no purpose to hold a grudge for something they probably couldn't help and might not even be aware of.

She clutched his arm tighter. "You need to let it go, hon."

"Why do you always have to be so right?" he asked, smiling down at her as she looked up at him. "That fuzzy red hat is ridiculous. Where'd you get it?"

She reached up and tugged it down in back. "Eric gave it to me for Christmas. Gloves, too."

"It's not Christmas for a couple of weeks yet. He's jumping the gun."

"Always does that, he says. Can't wait for the party."

"I'll have to go him one better. How about emeralds?"

She hummed the way she often did when considering something. "Like 'em fine. My birthstone. Little expensive for an office gift, don't you think?"

"But not for an engagement ring."

She stopped walking and pulled her arm from his. "Uh-uh, don't you do this!"

"Do what?" he asked, knowing she was about to throw the clumsy, impulsive proposal right back in his face.

"Don't you propose to me in the middle of a cemetery, that's what!"

He nearly sagged to his knees with relief. It was just the place. "Okay. Big production later, I promise."

She bobbed her head up and down emphatically. "Yeah! Way later and after you sober up. Nobody said a word about getting married."

"It was just a thought."

"I told you I don't do the games, Will. I don't know how to play, all right? I never dated in high school, only twice in college, and after that it was too late to learn. One very brief affair, a train wreck you've already heard about. That was my fault, okay? I don't do the games," she repeated, then took off.

"Fine. No games," he promised, catching up to her, freezing inside as well as out.

"How'd you get here?" he asked.

"Taxi. I had hoped to ride back with you. You want me to now?" She sounded a little worried, as if things had not gone quite as she'd planned.

"Sure, why not?"

"We'll stop off at Christa's for a beer," she informed him.

"Doing the *friend* thing up right, huh?"

"You bet. We need to get us back on an even keel." She threaded her arm through his again and made a dismissive little gesture with her free hand. "Get rid of this damn tension that's making us crazy."

"I only know one way to do that, and I think Christa would throw us out on our ears if we made love in a corner booth."

Again Holly stopped and turned on him, her face a study in frustration. And longing. "I do *not*—repeat, *not* intend to…" She threw up both hands and slapped them against her coat. "Oh, all right then, my place."

She didn't exactly sound overjoyed at the prospect

of falling into bed with him. Instead she seemed dismayed by her inability to tell him to go to hell.

"Sounds like a game to me, but okay," he said.

Not another word passed between them until they were back in McLean and almost to her apartment. Will wasn't sure he wanted this to follow through to the natural conclusion. Making love would definitely be another mind-blowing experience, but they still wouldn't have settled anything. Somehow he had to convince her that they loved each other enough to work this out. But could they really?

At least it would bring them closer together and in a more relaxed frame of mind. Maybe then some solution would magically occur.

Who was he kidding? There would be no magical answer. If they planned to continue, married or as lovers, one of them would have to leave the team, and he knew very well which one it would be. He could never ask that of Holly and expect her not to resent him for it, even if she were willing.

"I'll give it up," he said. Damn, what was he thinking? He hadn't meant to broach the subject yet. Not before...

"Give up what?"

"The job. I can go back to ATF. There's a vacancy." He added a forced smile to show he was good with it.

"No!" she protested.

"We'll talk about it later," he said, driving into her garage.

He had made up his mind. When it came to choosing between making her his and working for Sextant, his choice would always be Holly. And that was precisely why he knew his resigning would be for the best.

What kind of operative would he be if he couldn't put his team first? A dangerous one, and if she felt the same about him, so would she.

Holly unlocked her door and entered the apartment first, her mind torn by Will's declaration. She couldn't let him quit. But she had to admit that, deep down, she was tempted.

Hadn't she struggled for a position like this all her life? She had worked her butt off, sacrificed, all but clawed her way out of poverty to get where she was. Will had sailed along on family money, scholarships and personal recommendations, making his rise seem almost effortless.

No, that was not fair. Will would never have made it without his superior intelligence and giving all he had every step of the way. Despite the good ol' boy network that helped fill a lot of government positions, the Sextant team had been chosen with only their individual record of achievement and unique abilities in mind. They were the best.

She was proud of herself, but she was just as proud of Will. She knew he felt the same way. How could she deprive the team of him by agreeing to this?

"I can't let you do it," she announced, angrily peeling off her gloves. She snatched off her cap and shrugged out of her coat, tossing everything on a chair. "We end this here and now. Today. It's over." She plopped down on the sofa and kicked off her shoes.

Will had already gone to the bar and was pouring them a drink. "Sorry. That's not going to happen."

"I have a choice!" she argued, pointing her finger downward for emphasis. "If I say it ends, then it ends."

He turned and looked at her, a sad smile on his face as he walked over and handed her a Scotch. "No, I don't think you do have a choice in this, and neither do I. You love me and I love you. Inconvenient as that might seem, it's *not* going away."

They stared at each other for a full minute until her eyes began to water. Oh God, she was not going to cry. She turned away.

"This is a hell of a situation, isn't it? People in love are supposed to be thrilled about it. Here we are drinking to drown our sorrows." She gulped a swallow and smacked the glass down on the end table. "And it's not helping!"

Will laughed and sat down beside her, then leaned over and pressed his lips to hers. "I know something that should."

She lay back, rested her head against the pillows and closed her eyes. "Oh Will, what are we going to do?"

"I think you know. If you don't, I'll be glad to surprise you." He slid his hand upward from where it rested on her waist.

"You know this won't solve a thing," she warned.

"It won't change anything, either," he told her seriously. "Whether I ever touched you again or not, even if we went our separate ways and never saw each other, I would always feel the way I do now. I'll love you. I'll put you first, anyway. So you see, making love to you won't make any difference as far as that's concerned. Just accept it, Holly." His gaze caught hers and held. "Accept me."

"Oh, for goodness sake, just hold me, will you?" she cried. Really cried, which was something she never did. "Promise you'll respect me in the morning."

His shoulders shook with silent laughter. "Holly,

what are you talking about? We've already made love and you know I have the greatest respect for you."

"Not because of that," she said, sniffing. "I didn't want you to see me...like this. Crying like some stupid little girl."

"You aren't stupid by a long shot," he told her. "And you're certainly no little girl." He kissed the tears off her cheeks and tasted salt when he moved to her lips.

Seasoned with happiness and tears. The phrase from some song or other ran through her mind as they kissed. Something soft and sweet about passing years. She longed for years with Will, lots of them.

Holly knew he was right about the love. It was fated or something, unavoidable. She couldn't pretend to be sorry about that any longer.

She wanted him desperately, more than anything else in her life. Certainly more than any career, great as it was. Later, she would tell him that, assure him that he need not give up anything for her. She would be the one. She wanted to do it. For him, the most unselfish man she had ever met in her life.

All this...mine, she thought, reveling in the feel of his mouth on her skin. His deep-throated hum of pleasure vibrated through her breast, now bare to his touch. Those clever fingers of his worked fast, though he seemed to be taking his time getting down to business.

"Hurry," she urged, trying to reach between them for his belt.

He took her hand away, pushing it above her head and releasing it. "We have all night," he growled, his voice still low and dark with desire. "To do this...and this..."

Holly gave herself up to his inventiveness and, man,

was he ever creative. "For such a...straightforward guy...you certainly do travel the circuitous route... very well," she gasped. And shuddered with delight when he touched her with his tongue.

"Lovely landscape it is, too," he remarked, immediately returning to his travels.

Holly prayed for patience, but blood was singing through her veins, most of it rushing south.

He moved up and over her, entering her slowly, too slowly. When they were fully joined and as close as a man and woman could get, he paused and looked down into her eyes. "Only you, Holly...forever," he whispered, his hands cradling her face, thumbs brushing the tears away.

"Only you," she promised. "I love you, Will."

He moved languidly, drawing out the ecstasy almost to the point of pain for the longest time, until they could bear the delay no longer.

His breath rushed out hard and fast as he thrust deeply, each foray a claim on her very soul. She met him, urging him on, promising him everything she was or ever hoped to be. And his hot smoky gaze never left hers. His dark-fringed eyes, their deep gray irises nearly as dark as the dilated pupils, shone with purpose and promise and pleasure.

"Now?" he rasped.

Holly let herself fly free, exhilaration flooding her with wave after wave of incredible feeling. The descent lasted longer, interspersed with wonderful aftershocks that he seemed to relish as much as she did.

After a while, they lay perfectly still, replete. Untroubled. No matter what happened, she would always have this, Holly thought to herself. At this moment, she felt loved. He knew her better than anyone ever had before, faults and all, and right now he loved her just the way she was.

Holly woke alone at nine the next morning. They had gone to bed around six-thirty in the evening, but hadn't had a lot of sleep through the night. Will had probably gone back to his place for a change of clothes.

This was Wednesday and she'd taken the day off. He would be back soon, she was sure.

However, when one o'clock rolled around and she hadn't heard from him, Holly began to worry. Maybe he had changed his mind. She should have told him that she'd be willing to leave Sextant and let him stay. Or could it be that Will had decided this wasn't worth pursuing, after all?

She knew her own commitment issues stemmed from the only guy she had been with before him trying to make her over into something she wasn't. Easy enough to dismiss, now that she knew Will would never attempt such a thing. He loved her without wanting to change her. Didn't he?

Will's fear of emotional entanglement went a lot deeper than hers and would be much more difficult to overcome. It had to do with his mother and her virtual rejection of him, Holly figured. Yep, that would take a little therapy on her part, but she was trained for it.

By the time her phone rang, she was pacing the floor, her self-confidence trading blows with her anger. She snatched up the receiver. "Amberson," she snapped.

"Is Will there?" Jack asked.

"No, but when he does show up, he'd better be packing three dozen roses and a box of chocolate or he's dead meat."

There was a long pause.

"I'd like to see you both. Christa's at two and don't be late." He hung up.

"Christa's at two and don't be late," she mimicked to the dial tone. The instant she plunked down the receiver, her doorbell rang. She stalked barefoot to the door and flung it open. "What?"

"Hey," Will said.

"Where have you been?" she demanded. "Do you know how worried I've been?"

He shrugged. No expression. "Out," he said, a cryptic tone in his voice.

Holly realized she had sounded just like one of those horrible parodies of a nagging wife. Great impression to make. Yeah, he looked really entranced by her. "Sorry. How was your morning?"

Now he smiled. "Successful, I think. May I come in without fear of getting my throat ripped out?"

She stepped aside and gestured, her smile fake, her words loaded with sarcasm. She was still mad at him for deserting her before daylight. "Be my guest. Please. Could I get you anything?"

"Do you have champagne?" he asked politely.

She narrowed her eyes. "You should have brought some with you, cheapskate."

He pulled out one pants pocket to show it was empty. "Blew it all. I'm broke."

"Blew it on what?"

He pulled something out of his other pocket and opened his hand to show her. "This."

She felt her eyes go round as she stared at the black velvet ring box. "It's not."

"Yes, it is." He opened the box and left it sitting there for her to observe. It was a square-cut emerald surrounded by diamonds. The most beautiful ring in the world. "Well?"

Holly covered her mouth, too overcome to say anything.

"Don't leave me standing in your entry hall with my heart hanging out. Will you or won't you?"

She nodded so vigorously it made her dizzy. He was taking her left hand. He was sliding the ring on her third finger. And he was kissing her madly. Holly kissed him back.

He swung her around and carried her into the living room where he sat down with her on his lap. "So, what do you think? Can we get a wedding together by Christmas Eve? We could fly to Vegas."

"Not on your life. I want the whole shindig. White gown, couple of attendants in ugly taffeta dresses and you in a monkey suit. You're not sliding by with an elopement."

"Whatever you want," he promised with a quick kiss. "What else? Honeymoon in Hawaii?"

"And foot the bill by myself? You just said you were broke." She held her hand out to admire her ring again.

"I lied. I've got a little put by. See if you can swing a week or so between assignments." He started nibbling on her neck.

She pushed away. "What about that? You think he would let us both off at the same time?"

Will fiddled with the buttons on her shirt to avoid her eyes. "I quit. I went by and left my resignation."

She bolted upright. "You did what? What—what did he say?"

"Nothing. He was busy working on something. I gave it to him and left."

Ah. Now Jack's call made sense. She bit her lip for a minute before telling Will. "He called and said for us to come to Christa's at two. Bet I can guess what this is all about."

Will glanced at his watch. "Well, looks like we have almost an hour to kill. Want to play doctor?"

Reluctantly she pushed herself off his lap and got her balance. "As tempting as that sounds, I think we need to get down to the pub and get this over with."

"It is over, Holly. I'm out. I called Jim Ferguson at ATF and I can start the first of February."

"No."

He refused to discuss it. Holly might as well have been talking to a wall. She'd had no idea he was this hardheaded. How in the world could she convince Jack to keep him at Sextant and let her go if Will was determined not to stay? When the new wore off their marriage, Will would begin to regret what he had lost. She just knew it. If the situation did reverse, would she?

"You might want to get dressed," he advised. "Christa's not all that fussy, but she does require customers to wear shirts and shoes."

Christa Hart herself greeted them at the door. The busty blonde with a beautiful smile and jokes that could turn the air blue always welcomed them like family. It was rumored she'd had a wild fling with Jack back in the days when he was still with NSA.

Holly gave her a hug, then hurried on in ahead of Will to get to Jack first. She hoped to suggest her alternate plan for leaving Sextant herself before Will could get there, but he was right behind her.

The place, usually closed on Wednesdays, was

empty except for Christa and the team. Jack was waiting at the big round table where they always sat. Joe,
Clay and Eric were present, too. They had obviously
been there awhile. Empty pie plates and coffee cups
indicated a premeeting meeting.

An unusually silent Christa brought two more cups
of coffee, then disappeared into the back of the pub.

Holly pushed her coffee away. "We've been discussed, I take it?"

"Here's the deal," Jack announced, sliding a legal-
size envelope in front of Will. "First, shred that when
you get home. Second, I make the rules and it's not
against any rules of mine to have a couple on the team.
But you won't partner on a field op again unless we
go in as a crew of five. Agreed?"

Holly nodded, grabbing Will's hand for support.
This was going to work. It was going to *work!*

"Third, no communication except through control
center when one of you goes into the field alone.
Agreed?"

"Absolutely," Holly said. "Goes without saying."

"No it doesn't. I want that very clear. Any problems
come up, I need to know about them before they get
out of hand. You plan to part company, you keep it
civil. I don't want any personal friction screwing up
our team."

Will spoke up before Holly could get a word in this
time. "There's already a built-in problem that I identified in the resignation letter. Holly is and always will
be my first concern. That alone could endanger the others if we go en masse."

"Hasn't she always been first concern?" Jack asked.
He looked at Clay. "What about you? Who would you
rescue first in a life-threatening situation?"

"Holly. She's female."

"I resent that chauvinistic attitude!" Holly exclaimed. "And it assumes I'm not as capable as the rest of you. It's insulting!"

"That's the way it is," Clay said, fiddling with his coffee spoon.

"And you, Joe, how about it?" Jack asked before Holly could object further.

"Holly. She makes the best coffee and brings us homemade goodies. She's my favorite."

"Glutton," Holly said, rolling her eyes. "Say that in front of Martine and see how fast you can duck."

"Eric?"

"Holly. Sorry, guys, but she's a lot prettier than you."

"I cannot believe this! All this time, I thought you were treating me as an equal and now I find out you're nothing but a bunch of patronizing, dim-witted, politically incorrect...*men!*"

"And we all love you, too," Jack assured her. "Will just loves you more. You good with all this, Will?"

"I can handle it. Thanks, Jack." Holly felt him squeeze her hand, either communicating his excitement or warning her to shut up.

Eric snorted. "Yeah, Will, but can you handle *her* is what I want to know."

Holly bristled. "He handles me just fine, smart mouth. You need a spanking."

Jack stood up. "Come on, guys, we need to get out of here and leave these two to make some plans." He looked pointedly at her hand. "Nice ring."

She smiled up at him, forgiving him everything, now and in the future. "Nice man."

They left without ceremony as they always did.

Holly watched them go. "We are so damn lucky," she said with a sigh.

"And about to get even luckier," Will told her. He held up a key ring she hadn't seen before and rattled the keys. "Before she left, Christa asked me to lock up. You want to go neck in the back booth?"

"Will Griffin, you bad, bad man! When did you get so reckless?"

"Comes from getting shot in the head, I guess. Makes you do all kinds of strange things."

"Strange things, huh? You promise?"

"I promise."

Epilogue

"You do know how to throw a wild wedding, Mrs. Griffin." Will clinked his champagne flute against hers. They had said their vows in the chapel at St. John's, here in McLean, with two hundred in attendance. Ivory satin sculpted Holly's gorgeous figure like the hand of Michelangelo. Her face glowed with a happiness Will hoped he had helped put there.

She scanned the church's beautifully decorated social hall as she sipped her bubbly. "Your reception's not too shabby, either. And the honeymoon! I can't wait to get to Jamaica."

"I wish your mother could have seen you today."

"Yeah, me, too." She sighed happily and pointed across the room. "Would you look at this crowd! Eric's with Bev Martin, did you see? Isn't she a knockout?" And also too famous to be involved with an intelligence agent. Holly could see heartache coming when their occupation forced them to part company. But who was she to make predictions? Eric was the psychic and he should know what to expect. "He's way out of his league."

Will sipped, then wrinkled his nose at the fizzy champagne he hated. "I wonder if she realizes he knows exactly what she's thinking every minute,"

"*So* not fair. But without that clairvoyance of his, he'd be just another Brad Pitt look-alike. Smug rascal. Oh look, the fool's laying one on her right there on the dance floor!" Holly giggled. Maybe it *would* work out, after all.

"Smitten like me," Will told her, stealing a kiss himself. "By the way, did you have a chance to talk to your grandparents yet?" he asked softly, watching her eyes for a sign that she had suffered any insults. He would feel so responsible if she had. It had been at his insistence that she'd sent them a letter and an invitation.

"Muffie and Hank? Oh, they're simply *darling* people, you know," she gushed with a sly wink. "They flew in last night while you were yukking it up with the boys at your bachelor party."

"Well, don't keep me hanging. What happened?"

"At least they came. And I believe they're unbending a little. They gave us a nice toaster."

"A *toaster?*" he groaned as she laughed merrily. "For real?"

"Don't expect too much too soon. But we do have an invitation to their annual barbecue in July." She tapped a pearl-pink fingernail on his cheek. "And you, my man—what about your parents?"

He smiled down at her and flicked her veil off her

shoulder with the back of his hand. "They are happy for us. Really, they seemed very sincere." He looked at the well-wishers surrounding them, friends, fellow agents, relatives he hardly knew.

"You miss Matt today." Her wistful brown eyes teared up, making them glisten.

He knew it was for him.

No bride needs to cry sad tears on her wedding day. Do something!

Will shook his head. "Are you kidding? He and I were just having a great conversation in my head about the future as I was waiting for you to walk down the aisle. You sure took your time, by the way."

She looked at him askance, tilting her head the way she did when he was teasing her. "And what did he have to say?"

"How would you feel about having twins one day?"

"So you're getting messages from the beyond again? Well, you can tell that erstwhile brother-in-law of mine that he can jolly well get out of your head for the honeymoon. And he'd better leave any progeny predictions to us."

Will looked heavenward. "Little Wilhemena and Matilda, I can see them now. Two peas in a pod."

"Hey, this is the pod speaking. Five years down the road," Holly assured him, holding up her hand and wiggling her fingers. "Five. Not a day sooner."

Will shrugged. "He didn't specify when." He took their glasses and set them on a table, swept her into his arms to dance as the band struck up something with a slow, sweet sax.

She frowned up at him as the last long note of the

song sounded. "You *were* just joking, right? Matt didn't really...did he? Twins?"

Will whirled her around and dipped her, kissing her on the lips as their audience applauded madly.

Laughter echoed in his head. *I'm outta here...*

* * * * *

*Be sure to watch for more romances
in the Special Ops Series, coming only to
Silhouette Intimate Moments in 2005.*

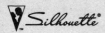

INTIMATE MOMENTS™

presents the continuing saga of the
crime-fighting McCall family

by favorite author

Maggie Price

Where peril and
passion collide.

Available in
December 2004:

Shattered Vows

(Intimate Moments #1335)

Lieutenant Brandon McCall is facing his toughest
assignment yet—to protect his estranged wife from
an escaped killer. But when the investigation forces
Brandon and Tory into close quarters, old passions are
revived—and new dangers threaten to destroy them.

*Look for the next book in this exciting miniseries, coming
in June 2005 to Silhouette Bombshell:*

TRIGGER EFFECT (#48)

Available at your favorite retail outlet.

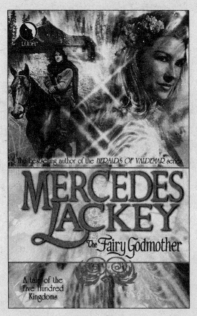

Coming in December 2004

The Scent of Lavender
series continues with

Jennifer Greene's

WILD IN THE MOMENT

(Silhouette Desire #1622)

The whirring blizzard, the cracking fire and their
intimate quarters had Daisy Campbell and
Teague Larson unexpectedly sharing a wild
moment. The two hardly seemed like a match
made in heaven...so why couldn't Daisy turn
down Teague's surprise business deal and
many more wild moments?

The Scent of Lavender

The Campbell sisters awaken to passion
when love blooms where they least expect it!

Available at your favorite retail outlet.

Silhouette®

INTIMATE MOMENTS

#1333 BENEATH THE SURFACE—Linda Turner
Turning Points

Crime reporter Logan St. John had sworn to protect Abby Saunders from her shady boss. But when Logan asked the innocent beauty on a date in order to investigate, he hadn't counted on falling for her! Soon a cover-up that could get them both killed was revealed, and Logan wondered if their newfound love would end before it even began….

#1334 RUNNING SCARED—Linda Winstead Jones
Last Chance Heroes

When a government official asked elite mercenary Quinn Calhoun to rescue Olivia Larkin from a ruthless dictator, he couldn't turn his back on the caring teacher. But an injury detained Cal and Livvie in the jungle, and passion flared between them. Could their growing love save them from the enemy, or would betrayal tear them apart?

#1335 SHATTERED VOWS—Maggie Price
Line of Duty

Lawman Brandon McCall had long since given up on his marriage to fiercely independent Tory DeWitt. Stubborn, beautiful Tory had never been willing to put her trust in Bran. But when he discovered an escaped convict's plan to exact revenge by harming Tory, he vowed to protect her at any cost—and win back her heart in the process.

#1336 DEADLY INTENT—Valerie Parv
Code of the Outback

Ryan Smith was the one man Judy Logan couldn't forget. After years away from her childhood crush, she now trusted him with the most important mission of her life—locating documents that could lead her to her family's fortune. But Ryan was keeping secrets, and the truth threatened to destroy their newfound love.

#1337 WHISPERS IN THE NIGHT—Diane Pershing

He'd been framed and sent to jail four years ago, but now Paul Fitzgerald was finally free—and getting close to Kayla Thomas was the only way to prove his innocence. But he hadn't counted on his attraction to the beautiful widow. He was determined to keep their relationship professional, until Kayla began receiving deadly threats, and he realized he would do anything to protect her.

#1338 DANGEROUS MEMORIES—Barbara Colley

Hunter Davis couldn't remember anything except an address in New Orleans and the face of a beautiful woman. So when he showed up at Leah Davis's door, she couldn't believe the husband who'd supposedly died five months ago was still alive. Could they rebuild their trust and find love again, or would Hunter's resurfacing memories cause Leah to lose him a second time?

SIMCNM1104